JEREMY GAVRON

The Book of Israel

Scribner

First published in Great Britain by Scribner, 2002
This edition published by Scribner, 2003
An imprint of Simon & Schuster UK Ltd
A Viacom Company

Copyright © Jeremy Gavron, 2002

Scribner and design are trademarks of Macmillan Library Reference USA,
Inc., used under licence by Simon & Schuster, the publisher of this work.

1 3 5 7 9 10 8 6 4 2

Simon & Schuster UK Ltd
Africa House
64–78 Kingsway
London WC2B 6AH

Simon & Schuster Australia
Sydney

www.simonsays.co.uk

A CIP catalogue record for this book is available from the British Library

ISBN 0-7432-2099-4

Typeset by M Rules
Printed and bound in Great Britain by
Cox & Wyman Ltd, Reading, Berks

For my families

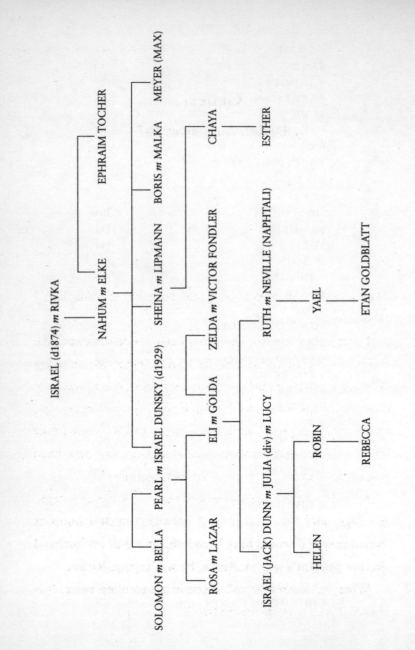

Genesis

Dunsk, Lithuania, 1874

The truth lies between God and your grandfather but I know what I know.

I was in the kitchen chopping carrots when I heard the cries. Your grandfather did not have a day of illness in his life before that afternoon. For twenty years every evening when he came home from the mill I had warm food on the table for his supper. Hot soups with cold sour cream. Meat stew with eyes of fat looking up at you. Bread steaming from the stove with as much goose fat as he could spread.

I put down the knife and went to the door. It was Joseph, your grandfather's assistant, if he wasn't such a lump of wood maybe it would have been him instead of my husband in that peasant's wagon. Rivka, he was crying, Rivka.

When he saw me he called out in a trembling voice, It is Israel, Rivka, I am bringing Israel.

They were coming up the path from the river, Joseph wading through the mud, his hand holding onto the wagon beside him, and what I thought looking at that long narrow wagon was it looked like a grave. If I still had the knife in my hand I would have plunged it into my heart.

Praise to God I didn't, the next moment from inside the wagon an arm lifted up. Your grandfather was alive, but as near dead as a man can be and not lie wrapped in his burial shroud. He was sweating even in the cold, and his skin was paler than the flour dust in his beard. The look on his face I will never forget, if he wasn't my own husband I would have run from the dybbuk I thought must be in him. He was tearing at the shirt on his chest and when I reached to stop him he gripped my hand so tight I thought my fingers would break.

What are you standing there for, I told Joseph and the idiot wagoner. Take him into the house.

We'll carry him like a baby, Joseph said.

They put him on his bed, and I sent Joseph to bring him a glass of tea, but he wouldn't drink. He kept groaning and clutching his chest; when I asked what was wrong he only stared at me with those terrible eyes. I cried to God that he had abandoned us, and perhaps he was listening a little, for after a time Israel's breathing calmed. I tried him with tea again, but he closed his eyes and went to sleep.

He slept through my taking off his coat and pulling the shirt from his shoulders and bathing his face with warm water. It was the only time in his life he didn't wash the flour away himself. Every evening he would stop at the barrel by the door and dip those big hands like spades into the water and splash his face. I can still remember the first day he came home from the mill. Your father was a small boy, not even at school yet. He ran into the kitchen shouting, Mameh, Mameh, the Messiah is coming. Well, he must come at some time to some place, and why not our little town? I wiped my hands and took off my apron and barely stopping to straighten the scarf on my head hurried after him to the door. There was the Messiah walking up the same path Joseph brought him in that wagon. With his black beard white with flour Nahum didn't recognize his own father.

Israel barely had a hair of that beard the first time I saw him. We were children when we married. It was Tsar Nikolai's terror, catchers banging on your door in the middle of the night to take any boys not yet espoused to serve in the unholy army. Half a lifetime they kept them, if the enemies' swords didn't kill them, or they didn't give up their faith and marry Gentiles. The ones who came back were broken, like Wolf the graveyard keeper who sleeps with the ghosts.

My hips and bosom had barely started to swell against the seams of my dress when the matchmaker came to drink tea with my father. They talked into the night and the next morning my father told me, Congratulations, you are engaged. On my wedding night I took my doll to bed with me. It was a year before I could look my husband in the face, another before I had my first son I lost.

I unrolled a feather bed on the floor of his room and lay down in my clothes. It was the first time in all our years I stayed a whole night alone in a room with him. I lay on that bed with my eyes open and listened to the noises he was making. It was like he was praying in his sleep, strange prayers I had never heard before. If I slept myself it was a minute. What woke me was his silence and a stone lay on my heart until he snorted and his breathing started up again.

Everything I could I did. I put salt and pepper in his pockets and hung amulets over his bed. On every window and door I made Joseph write with a piece of chalk, The Jew Israel Does Not Live Here, so the Angel of Death would pass by. I went to the cemetery and called to Israel's dead who lay there to help him. He wouldn't eat, but if I held a spoonful of soup or a glass of tea to his lips he would sip a little. Other things I had to do for him also. He was too weak to get out of bed. He was helpless like you, little one.

In the morning Yankel the feldsher came with his cups to draw out what was inside him. When that didn't make him any better I sent Joseph to bring old Zlate, whose hands pulled your father from my belly, and would have pulled you from your mother's if you hadn't been so impatient. She came with her wax and poured it into water while she said her spells against what I told her I had seen in Israel's face. That afternoon he sat up and drank a whole bowl of soup and I thought he was going to get well again, but in the night he started shivering and didn't stop even with the stove next to him and three feather quilts on him. I told Joseph, enough, he must go and bring the doctor, whatever Israel always said about non-kosher bones in his house.

It took two days for the doctor to come. It seemed he had forgotten that his mother and father were Jews. His chin was as bare as his head and his coat barely covered his shirt. He knocked on Israel's ribs and looked in his mouth. When he took out a snake I thought he was going to feed it down Israel's throat to bite the dybbuk and kill it, but he put it into his own ears and pressed it to Israel's chest. His fee was a week's profit from the mill but the draft he wrote didn't help any more than the blood he let from Israel's hands, though enough came out to colour the Red Sea.

Where is my son? Israel kept asking. I told him I had sent a letter, Nahum would come as soon as he could. Most of what he said I couldn't understand. He talked more in his sleep than when he was awake, mostly Hebrew or some spirit language. One time he opened his eyes and reached for me. For a long time he held my hand and looked in my face. I don't know if his strength was all gone but his fingers were like silk on mine. I never knew a man could be so gentle.

God forgive me for sinning, our life together wasn't

always licking honey. When he brought me to this town we lived with his family in one room. I slept on the stove with his grandmother. On Fridays they sent me to bed early and put up a sheet for a curtain and he came to me. Such a rib cage he had beneath his vest, when his bones pressed on me I thought I would burst. The next night I would feel the old woman's cold claw on my belly to see if I was growing.

Your father and grandfather walked across half the country buying anything they could find a little cheap in one village and selling it for a few kopeks more in the next. The old woman baked bagels while they were gone and sold them at kitchen doors. We lived on next to nothing and half of that the Tsar took. A tax for bread, a tax for chimneys, one year he even passed a tax for earlocks. When the tax men came to collect they brought a dog the size of a bear so you couldn't say no. Even the beast was a Jew-hater. If you forgot to close your window it would lift its leg and spoil what you had on your stove.

Only when the old Tsar died could we breathe a little easier. When the mill came free Israel borrowed some rubies and grabbed his luck with the lease. He built this house to be near the river, with wooden floors to keep out the damp and a second roof, like the skullcap he wore under his hat when he went out, in case the wind should lift off what was on top.

If there had been ten Jews like your grandfather in Sodom it would be standing now. If he committed a sin even by accident he spent a whole day praying for God's mercy. Every night he stayed up studying his sacred books until the wax from the candles was so thick on the pages he could hardly see the words and the books were so swollen he had to build new shelves to hold them all.

At least he saw you that one time.

More than once I thought he was going to leave me, but he wasn't ready yet. That's when I thought maybe it wasn't a dybbuk, dybbuks don't let you choose your time.

The mill had been closed for a week. The snow came and Joseph took the wheel from the river. I stuffed paper into the cracks in the walls and stoked up the stove next to his bed and wondered when your father would come. I didn't think he would bring your mother in her condition.

I was blowing out the candles when I heard the sound of a horse over the silence of the snow. The shutters were closed, so I opened the door and saw the wagon.

Do I have to say kaddish? your father asked.

He still lives, God protect us from the evil eye, I told him. Then I saw your mother up on the box, swaddled in blankets like she was a baby herself. Why are you asking questions when your wife is freezing to death in the snow? I told him. For God's sake bring her in.

Nahum went to see your grandfather while I took Elke into the kitchen and set the samovar boiling for some hot tea. If it was the warmth after the cold or just her time had come early I don't know, but the next thing I knew she was moaning. I sent Nahum back into the snow to fetch old Zlate and prayed to God to give me strength. Alone in the house with your grandfather lying between life and death and your mother pumping water all over the kitchen floor, I had your head in my hands when old Zlate came.

You would have thought all the noise would wake the dead, but Israel slept through that night. In the morning when I brought you to him his eyes were his own. They smiled that you were a boy.

Then his brow furrowed, like when he read his holy books, peering at the words through the wax.

I need to talk to the Rabbi, he said.

The Rabbi will come on the eighth day, I told him. Rest, you will need your strength to hold him at the circumcision.

I want the Rabbi, he said. Bring the Rabbi.

With the snow, and all I had to do, washing the blood from you, hanging the sheets around Elke's bed, it wasn't until the afternoon that I could go to bring the Rabbi. He didn't want to come, it was snowing, he had a chill himself, it could wait, but I told him death doesn't wait.

He drank two glasses of tea straight down when we came in, and took another into your father's room. It was men's talk, but what if the door was open a little and the house was quiet with the baby sleeping and the snow?

It's cold out there, Rabbi? I heard Israel ask.

It's cold.

It's not so warm in here.

The stove was by his bed and he had three feather quilts on him, but still he was cold.

Rabbi, he said, I have a question for you.

Through the crack in the door I saw the Rabbi take the sugar lump from his mouth.

So ask, he said.

Only a dead man can pass his name to a child? Israel whispered.

This you have to ask? the Rabbi said.

I could not see Israel, only the Rabbi, but I heard what your grandfather said. What if the man is alive when the boy is born and dead before he is named?

The Rabbi put the sugar lump back between his teeth and sipped his tea and was silent for a long time.

This is an interesting question, he said.

We waited, your grandfather and I, either side of that door. It seemed a day and a night before the Rabbi answered.

It is allowed, he said, but only if the man dies before the eighth day.

That week the river froze. They had to break the ground with axes. When it is spring, my little Israelke, I will take you to visit your grandfather.

Kings

Dunsk, 1880–1

What are you doing sitting with your hands idle, Israel? Do you think the King of the Universe does not see? He sees everything and judges everything. Now come and help with your father's boots. I have been standing all day at the mill. Not one minute have I been sitting with my hands idle.

Harder, you must pull harder, my feet are aching.

Now the other, pull, pull, the day does not stand still, do you want to be pulling when the Sabbath comes?

Ah, that is better. Now tell your mother to bring me a glass of tea, and when you have done that you can take my boots to polish them. And do not dawdle. You have already spent enough time this afternoon sitting with your hands idle.

–

What is this, Israel? What are you putting on my boots?

Elke! Where is my fish oil?

What smell? It smells of fish, that is all. Do my feet not trouble me enough without putting this rubbish waste of money polish on my boots? It does nothing for my boots, the fish oil feeds the leather, keeps it soft for my feet.

I am going to Baruch's if that is all right with you. I am going to borrow his fish oil while my feet can still carry me there, if his wife has not thrown it away because she does not like a little smell.

Come, Israel, I have finished sharpening the knife.

Look at these soft hands. The hands of a scholar. See your poor father's, how hard and cracked they are from threshing the grain and lifting sacks of flour. This is why you must not sit and daydream your life away. Do you want to grow up to work like a mule all your days? Look how my nails are broken even before I have a chance to pare them.

Do not fidget, the knife is sharp. We do not want these soft scholar's hands to get cut.

You remember the order for the left hand?

That is correct, never two fingers that are next to each other or the hearing can be impaired. God willing soon you will be studying these rules yourself.

Now the right hand. There, it is done. Take the nails

carefully to the stove, do not drop any. If you spill them and a pregnant woman walks over them and loses her baby it will be on your head.

Come, Israel, it is time to walk to the bath-house. Ah, taste the air. Is it not a sweet wind that blows in the Sabbath?

Turn your eyes away, Israel. We are coming to the place from where you can see the church.

Good afternoon, Reb Yankel. You have finished sweating already? It is hot inside? Come, Israel, take off your clothes so that we can go in and enjoy the heat.

Ah, it is nice and steamy in here. Is that you, Reb Shmeril? It is hard to see. God be with you.

Yes, this is the boy.

Come out from behind my legs, Israel. Reb Shmeril is talking to you.

Go on Israel, Reb Shmeril has asked you to recite what you have been studying this week. Recite something for Reb Shmeril. When you are finished you can take one of these branches and smite my back.

Let us go into the synagogue, Israel. Those boys can run around and use up all their energy for nothing. They are not fortunate like you. They have to sit at the back where they disturb each other. You are honoured to have your own seat next to your father in front of the Ark.

Stand aside, Israel, let the wagon pass.

Look at those poor peasant boys sitting on the wagon with their bare legs covered in dust while we are walking home from the beautiful service in our Sabbath suits. Has not God favoured us, for all our hardships?

Of course you may ask me a question Israel. Ask any question and I will answer you truthfully.

What kind of question is this? What are you talking that God should order me to sacrifice my own son?

Well I am not Abraham and you are not Isaac. This is an idiot question. I did not say you could ask idiot questions. And walk slowly, Israel, walking home for the Sabbath meal is a sacred duty and it is as sinful to hurry a sacred duty as it is to ask idiot questions.

Israel, go to see who is at the door.

There are some coins for him in the bowl.

You gave? Good. But have you not forgotten something? Old Solomon only has one arm. You must say the blessing for seeing a deformed person. Let us say it together. Blessed are you, Lord our God, King of the Universe, who varies the forms of his creatures.

That is better. Now bring me a handkerchief to put over my face, I cannot sleep for all these buzzing flies.

Feh, Elke! You know who was at the house of study tonight? Nachman's son, Hersh. He had a newspaper he brought from the city, he was reading it out aloud as if everybody who goes to pray to God wants to hear what is happening in St Petersburg or Paris. He was boasting to everyone that he reads a newspaper every day in the city. I told him here we read the Bible every day. That is our daily newspaper.

Yes, he still has a beard on his chin, though they say he folds it when he does business with Gentiles. Why he does not just shave it off I do not know. A beard without a Jew is worse than a Jew without a beard.

Come, Israel, let us go for our swim, if this burning sun has not dried up all the water in the river. Whoever says God makes laws only against doing things obviously does not know his holy books, for does it not say that a man should teach his son to swim? My father, bless his memory, taught me as I am teaching you. Have I told you how when I was a young boy I swam right across the river to the far bank?

Well you can hear it once more. Of course the river was wider in those days, the current was much stronger. When your grandfather saw me he was sure I would drown or if I did not drown I would be stuck on the far side, the police

14

would arrest me as a smuggler. When I swam back he slapped me so many times in the water I thought I was going to drown. But long after the pain from those slaps had gone he was still telling the story of his son's amazing swim.

Here we are, the water is still there.

Fold your clothes neatly, Israel. Do not scatter them on the ground like the other boys.

Wait, Israel. In this heat you must enter the water slowly or the shock can harm you or even kill you.

What does it matter who it killed? What matters is what your father tells you. Now this is far enough. We will stand here for a minute and let our feet adjust to the cold.

We can splash a little on our legs.

Now on the belly.

Now the arms and face.

Now the head. It is most important not to forget the head. You do not want to shock the head.

Now you can go in. On your side, that is right, bring your arm over your shoulder.

And do not go out too far.

Of course even I was nothing as a swimmer compared to Ber the fish. He could float absolutely still in the water with his hands above his head and one knee in the air. He was such a good swimmer he could cut his nails according to the laws while floating in the middle of the river. I saw it for myself on more than one occasion. He caught the parings on a piece of paper balanced on his knee. He would let us children inspect the paper to make sure he had not dropped any.

A glass of tea, Elke, my throat is parched from this heat.

Ah, that is better. Another glass, please.

I have never seen a summer like this. It is a month now and not a single drop of rain. If it does not rain soon the crops will shrivel up in the fields.

What do you think? The harvest will be ruined.

There will be no flour for the mill. You think you can get flour from a ruined harvest?

What will happen will happen. Do you think I am God? That is his will. He will provide.

You are late from school Israel. I was waiting to see you at home before I set off for the house of study. And why are you all covered in dust? And your head? Israel, your cap is not on your head. What have you done with your cap?

Yes, it is bare. You are walking naked through the town. You are walked naked like a slop bucket. Do you think this is why Moses the teacher led us out of bondage?

What is this Israel? Are you crying? It is I who should be crying that my son should walk naked.

Stop crying I said.

Stop or I will make you stop.

I have been

too

soft

on

you.

Now no more crying. A fine kaddish you are. Go now and find your cap and when you get home you can tell your mother to send you straight to bed without any supper. I am going to pray to God for forgiveness for your sins. And put your handkerchief on your head so it is covered.

Elke, I am back. Where is that son of yours? I hope he is in his bed without his supper.

What poor boy? What are you talking about?

Of course I asked him. I asked him ten times where his cap was but all the little bandit did was blubber.

He was crying because he lost his cap.

Don't ask me how. It was not me that lost my cap.

I am not shouting. If you want to hear me shouting I will do some shouting for you.

What condition?

No I did not know. How am I supposed to know? Am I Zlate the midwife? How can I know if you do not tell me?

So, it is good. Let us pray to God it is a boy.

Yes, yes, I will listen now.

You are sure?

This is an outrage. Something must be done about these Gentile dogs. I am going to talk to the fire committee about it. If anyone sees one of these beasts they can ring the fire bell, the men can come out and drive it away with sticks.

Israel, are you awake? Israel, Israel, it is your father.

Here, sit up.

Look what I have brought you.

Drink, drink the milk. Do you want a biscuit?

Israel, Sheina, be quiet, your mother is resting. Be quiet, I said, do you want your brother to be born deformed?

Elke, a glass of tea for my throat, I have swallowed so much flour today you could bake a loaf in my belly. The stones did not stop grinding for a minute, no thanks to the idiot peasants with their unthreshed grain. You know what we found in the grain today?

A finger.

Yes, if you can call these idiots human. It is bad enough what else they bring in their grain. Not only husk and straw but rocks that would damage the millstones, dead rats, droppings I only hope are from animals. You remember when Joseph found a pig's trotter in the grain? I had to go to the rabbi to get a dispensation for the mill. It was only because we thresh the grain for them that this finger did not get ground into flour. Where it came from God only knows, though half these peasants have fingers missing or extra ones. It is hard to believe they are descended from the same Adam.

Is this not a fine booth Elke? It is the best booth we have ever built. Look at the roof, Israel and I gathered the thickest, most luxurious pine branches from the forest, you cannot see a single star through this roof. I think we are going to have a beautiful week eating in this booth.

You are imagining things Elke. Why do you always have to think the worst? It is not going to rain tonight.

Eat your soup, children. Does not even the simplest food taste better when you eat it in the booth?

What raindrop? Even if it is raining a little outside, the rain cannot penetrate this roof. We could sleep the night in this booth in a storm and stay completely dry.

So one raindrop fell in your soup. One raindrop will not hurt you. Even the best roof will let in one raindrop. Now stop sinning, Elke, you are putting the children off their soup.

Go inside then. The children and I are staying. Could our forefathers in the desert on the way to the Promised Land go inside a nice house every time a few raindrops fell on their heads?

All right, take Sheina then. The men are staying here. Come Israel, eat your soup. A little rain never hurt anyone. It is nothing to eat in the booth when the weather is fine.

Israel, it is time to go to school.

This snow is not deep, Elke. I have known snow so deep in this town it covered even the roofs of the houses. One winter I remember we could not get out of the house for a week. We lived on what we had in the cupboard and drank water melted from the snow we scooped through the windows. Israel does not need to miss school for a few flakes of snow.

Come, Israel, bring the lamp, if it is as deep as your mother thinks I will carry you on my back.

We are not commemorating anything, Israel. On this day we do not go out of the house, that is all. Every winter after Hanukah there is a day like this. On this day the Jews close their shops and pray in their homes, that is all.

I think I will put some brandy in my tea. It is cold out there, the snow is deep. There was barely a minyan at the synagogue. Even Zorach the psalm-reader was not there. In thirty years I have never known Zorach the psalm-reader to miss a service at the synagogue.

–

Come, Israel, we will say the blessing together.

Blessed are you, the Lord our God, King of the Universe, for making this child a boy.

We are going to name him Boris, after your mother's brother, God rest his soul, who died when he was only a child. That is why it is important for a man to have more than one son. If something should happen to you, Israel, then I will still have Boris to say kaddish for me when I die.

Elke, another glass of tea for our guest. Bring some biscuits as well, some little cake for Reb Mottel, he has brought us good news. Elke, where are you? Reb Mottel the teacher has good news about Israel. Our son is to be a Gemara boy. Did you hear that Elke? Reb Mottel says Israel is ready to start studying the Talmud.

Come, Israel, sit and tell your father what you have been studying this week. I knew you would be a scholar from the first day you sat on my knee when you were a baby and pointed to the words on the pages I was reading in my holy book. Do you remember this?

I would put you on my knee. Every Sabbath afternoon when I read my holy books. Do you not remember?

What is that?

Oh, yes, you may start.

–

21

Ah, it is nice and steamy in here. Is that you, Reb Shmeril? It is hard to see. God be with you.

Yes, he is here, Reb Shmeril.

Yes this is the Gemara boy. Reb Mottel says it will not be too long before we have to start thinking about sending him away to theological college.

Answer Reb Shmeril, Israel. Tell him what you have been studying. Tell him about the case of a pig digging in a dunghill and causing something to fly out of it so that damage results therefrom that you have been studying. Tell Reb Shmeril what the law is in that case, Israel. And what payment must be made for poultry breaking utensils both directly with their wings and with the vibration from their wings. What do the Rabbis say about this, Israel? How much should the payment be? Tell Reb Shmeril what it says in Baba Kamma, Israel.

What are you doing out of bed, Israel? You should be sleeping so you have energy for your studying tomorrow.

Your mother is busy with the baby. You are a man not a little girl who needs her mother to kiss her goodnight. Do you not give thanks to God every morning in your prayers for not making you a Gentile or a girl?

They have found Zorach, Elke. This afternoon when Nissen came to the synagogue he saw a hand sticking out from the snow. A goat had been eating it. Poor Zorach must have slipped or suffered some illness as he came to the synagogue, and was buried by the snow. To think that he has been lying there all this time close enough to listen to others read the psalms as he so loved to do.

Come, everybody, it is time to go to synagogue for the reading of the Book of Esther. Sheina, where is your mother? Has she got Boris ready? Israel, do you have my prayer-book?

Come, let us go. We do not want to miss hearing how Esther marries the king and defeats the evil Haman and saves the Jews.

See how the snow melts. The King of the Universe has melted the snow in honour of Purim.

Sit still, Israel, do not look back at those boys making their noise with their rattles. These noises are for low-bred boys to make, not a Gemara boy who studies the laws concerning the breaking of a pitcher of water on public ground.

Why do you keep turning round?

Who is that? Who is this man coming into the synagogue without his head covered?

What is the stanovoy doing here?

Be quiet, Israel, I want to hear what the stanovoy is saying.

Dead? Who is dead?

The Tsar? The Tsar of all the Russias is dead? Tsar Alexander is killed?

So, the Tsar is dead. The King of the Universe still lives. Let us continue with the reading.

1 Judges

Northern Lithuania, 1886

The day in question we, Dugaev and me that is, were on our
way back from escorting a prisoner. A murderer he was,
looking at ten at least in Siberia, he stabbed a man over a
horse, though you wouldn't think it to see him. All bones
under his coat like a bird, but as they say even a small bird
has a sharp claw. We had him in jingles but we didn't need to.
He was no trouble. Sat in the cart, did as he was told, barely
said a word. We took him to where he had to go and got the
papers signed and were started back when the wheel of the
cart broke. Hit a stone and snapped in half. The nearest
wheelwright was five versts back, but the carter knew an inn
at a crossroads a couple of versts ahead and he said he'd take
the wheel back and get it fixed and meet us at the inn.

We found the inn all right. Not much of a place, Jew-
owned, like all the inns in these parts. There were no

customers when we arrived, only a Jew girl behind the counter, though her father appeared pretty quick. Seeing as we'd delivered our prisoner and looked like having to wait a time we didn't see why we shouldn't have a drink, so we got a bottle and asked for some food, and the Jew said he'd see what they had.

We sat and drunk our bottle. Not vodka, some piss they drink around here, nineties they call it, but at least it wakes up the throat. The Jew brought us bread and cucumbers, and said we could have calves' feet and soup later. The bread was alright but the cucumbers were watery and thick-skinned, and we concentrated on the drinking. We'd just ordered a second bottle when the soldiers came in. Four of them, Ukrainians they were. When I was in the army, Russians like myself wouldn't have given them the time of day, but out here at the end of the world with only Lithuanians and Polacks and Jews even a Ukrainian in the Tsar's uniform was a sight for sore eyes and I told them to sit with us and have a cup of our poison.

There wasn't a barracks around there; they'd been work-ing on the harvest, rented out by their colonel to some landowner like half the army when there isn't a war, and now the harvest was over they were returning to billets. Ukrainians are good drinkers, if nothing else, and we'd soon finished that second bottle and were onto another and were talking, as happens. I asked them if they'd seen any action, which they hadn't, and I told them how I'd been at Plevna with Skobeliov and they asked if it was true what they said, how the General rode ahead of the whole army. All true, I told them, I saw it with my own eyes, which I did. Bullets singing around him, one knocking off his hat, another killing his horse from under him. Up he jumped and grabbed another mount and rode on bareheaded. Not a bullet could touch him. We'd have followed him to hell after that, and I nearly did, or heaven, came within an inch of talking my last words to a Turkish sabre.

It was on that campaign I lost my finger. I had this old flintlock rifle, a terrible kick it had, my right cheek was always swollen and sore. Always misfiring too. One time it played up, so I cleaned the touch-hole, poured in some more powder, struck the flint, and what happened, the powder ignited but the gun didn't go off. In the thick of battle this was, too. Turks pouring down on us. My sergeant was screaming at me to fire, so thinking there might be some blockage I poked my finger into the barrel and that was when the gun went off. Not properly or it would have taken my whole hand, but enough to lose the finger. The doctor cut off what was left with scissors. A right tyrant that sergeant was. I'm God and the Tsar, he used to say, until he took a sabre in his belly.

The Jew finally bought our soup and the calves' feet, which tasted a bit Jewishy, but went down all the same, and when we'd wiped our bowls clean with bread one of the Ukrainians took out a pack of cards. It was starting to get on, so Dugaev went outside to see if there was any sign of the carter, but the road was empty, so we decided there was no harm in a quick game.

Three Leaves was the call, and I was happy with that, thought I might make a ruble or two, them being Ukrainian. I didn't expect them to turn out cheats. We called for another bottle of the Jew's best piss and stacked our coins in front of us and played. They must have been cheating because we were both up at first, Dugaev and me, but after that they bled us dry. When our own kopeks went we used our expenses money and when that was gone I pulled out the carter's payment, which we hadn't given him yet. It was the Jew's liquor that did it, and my trusting the Ukrainians on account of our talk about soldiering and Skobeliov and my war wound. They cleaned us out of every last quarter kopek, and when the table was empty in front of us and piled high in front of them I put my sheepskin down and when they won that too I knew what was what.

You're cheating, you villains, I said.

What us? they said all sly, and I didn't know why I hadn't seen it in their faces before.

Give us back our money, I told them, and Dugaev said that if they didn't we'd arrest them.

For what? one of them said. Playing cards and drinking with you when you are on duty?

That made me angry as hell, but I wasn't so far gone I couldn't see they were right. This stanovoy we work under is a right stickler for the rules.

We'll take it off you then, I said.

Come on, they said. Put up your fists and fight with them instead of your tongue.

They were standing by then, four big boys. I had them in experience and if I'd been ten years younger I might have taken them all, with Dugaev's help. But as it was, all I could do was watch them scoop up the money and pay the Jew who had been cowering in the corner and leave. I followed them to the door to hurl a few insults at them, and saw that it was dark. I don't know where they were going to sleep, and didn't care. I hope they froze, though it wasn't cold enough for that, and they had my coat, the warmest coat I ever had.

When I came back in the Jew had turned Jewish, was telling Dugaev it was late, he wanted to close up, could we pay him for the drink and food.

We'll pay you tomorrow, I told him. We're sleeping here if that's alright with you, or if it's not.

He didn't have much to say about that, except I watched him carry his money box with him from under the counter and heard the door lock behind him.

I stretched out on a table but I couldn't sleep. It was thinking about losing my coat that kept me awake, even more than the money or those cheating Ukrainians or the Jew piss that made me forget my sense. My wife gave me that coat the last time I went home, two years ago nearly it was. It's eleven years we've been married and barely two months I've had at home all that time. Neither a maiden nor a widow she is, as the song goes. I've got three kids, one from before the army, one from leave, and one from when I'd done my seven years.

I didn't intend to be a policeman, all through my army times I was itching to get home. Once a peasant, always a peasant. But when I'd earned my biscuit what was I going to do? Earn your biscuit – it's no joke. Two rubles ten kopeks a year is the pay in the army and when you're released a handful of biscuits. It was winter and I don't know how I made it home. So cold I saw a jackdaw freeze on the wing and fall out of the sky like a brick, and when I walked into my home half-dead from cold and hunger, even before I had a chance to say hello, my wife was searching through my pockets for money.

Fourteen desiatinas of land we have in my family, but that's divided between three brothers and hocked up to the neck. I can remember hunger as a boy when it didn't rain for two whole years. We had to eat acorns and grass, soup made from glue and water. But at least we were all in the same boat then, the master did what he could, opened his grain barns to feed us until they ran empty. And when there was plenty we all benefited. Those holidays when I was a boy! Buckwheat pies and green wine on the master's lawn. You had to bow and kiss his hand but who cared with a few glasses of wine down you, even us children, the steward filled every glass.

But now, now the corn grows and you have to sell it for money for the payments and village taxes and zemstvos and state taxes, and somehow the prices are always high when you need to buy and low when you want to sell. Before I left the village I thought that was just the way it was, but I'm not such a fool now. I learned to read and write in the army and I've been around. I've seen things. I know who controls the price of corn and flour and sucks the country dry.

The arrears would be growing with every year if my brother wasn't working in a factory and I wasn't a police-man posted out here in the middle of nowhere scraping by to send home four rubles a month, and sometimes a little beer I make here and there under the counter. Man is only human. I'd go back like a shot, if I could. If I won the lottery I'd buy that land outright and a little bit more and farm it like a gentleman. Sow my oats when the hickory blooms, make hay on St Peter's Day. Grow just enough to feed the family and pay the taxes and no more or they'll just up the taxes. In the spring there's mushrooms and berries to pick in the forests, and in the evenings vodka to drink and children and grandchildren eventually to watch. All paid up, the land will be in my family forever.

That's what I dream about to get myself to sleep at nights, and I must have nodded off in the end, because the next thing I knew I opened my eyes and the Jew was standing over me as if he was about to rob me with his grubby fingers. What are you doing? I shouted, jumping up, and then had to sit down again because someone was firing canons in my skull. The sly Jew brought me a glass of water, and another for Dugaev, who didn't seem in any better condition. We drank the water, and ate a little bread the Jew gave us.

Has the carter come? I asked the Jew, when my head stopped pounding so badly, and he said he hadn't seen or heard anyone.

We'd better go and look for him, I told Dugaev.

What about my money? said the Jew.

Money? I said. Money? I've half a mind to arrest you for trying to poison us with your pissy liquor. It's probably not even liquor, some kind of Jewish sleeping potion, I saw the way you were standing over us ready to rob us and probably would have done if the Ukrainians hadn't done it first. Come to think of it, how do we know you're not in league with them, that you didn't plan it all along, feed us your poison and let them fleece us?

That shut him up, though the mention of fleece made me think of my coat again. Come on, I said to Dugaev, who was staring at the Jew.

The morning air made me shiver, and I told Dugaev to hurry up and get walking.

We left the cart that way, he said.

Well he hasn't come, I said. How do we know he's going to come at all. He's probably pissed off somewhere on the drink. He's forfeited his right to be paid if you ask me. We can walk. It can't be more than twenty versts, and we'll get hell if we're not back today.

It wasn't only the cold, my feet were killing me. On eight rubles a month, four of which I send home, I can't buy anything but rubbish, and the soles had worn through on both feet.

Did you hear that bloodsucker? I said to Dugaev as I hobbled along. It's well known that Jewish innkeepers intoxicate the peasants on purpose to suck their money. I didn't see any Jews at Plevna, and those that were there were always skiving behind, medics and cooks and Jewishy jobs like that. Jewish exploitation is sucking the vital juices out of Russia.

Long-nosed garlic breaths, Dugaev said, they murdered our Tsar. We should have slaughtered them all when we had the chance back in eighty-one and eighty-two.

I was in the army then, I told him, they kept us in the barracks, I didn't get a chance to join in.

That was when we saw the Jew boy walking towards us along the path.

Where are you going? I asked him.

Home, he said.

Where are you coming from then? I asked him.

College, he said.

Well that's a filthy lie, I told him, Jews aren't allowed in colleges. The Tsar put a stop to that in his new laws.

It's a Jewish college, he said.

I know about those places, Dugaev said. That's where they teach all that Jewishy magic and spells, how to kill Christian boys and use their blood to make matzos.

We didn't hurt him much, just roughed him up a little, and I confiscated his coat. We're policemen, we have to uphold the law and morals. He wasn't dead. We saw him get up after we left him. I would have confiscated his boots as well, but they were too small, and anyway they had this horrible fishy smell.

Exegesis

Jewish theological college, Telz, Lithuania

Our property has been freely looted, our homes have been booty, our honour held cheap, our wives and children put to shame, and our lives have been at the mercy of the oppressor. Every Sunday, on every Christian holiday, dread fills us. We always ask: What will tomorrow bring?

Moses Leib Lilienblum, 1882

R. Samuel b. Nahmani said in the name of R. Jonathan: Blasted be the bones of those who calculate the advent of the Messiah. For they would say, since the predetermined time has arrived, and yet he has not come, he will never come. But wait for him, as it is written, Though he tarry, wait for him.

Babylonian Talmud

Everyone must ask: Why were the Jews so blind as not to see the evil coming? Why were they so complacent when the sword was being brandished before their faces? But the fact is that for many years our prophets so lulled us that we no longer saw reality and failed to anticipate the evil.

Perez Smolenskin, 1881

Why do we await the Messiah's coming? – To be rewarded for waiting, as it is written, Blessed are all they that wait for him.

Babylonian Talmud

Try, if only for one day, to free yourself from prejudices to which you have become accustomed from your childhood without your will and knowledge; try only for once to cast off blind faith in the authority of such ordinary persons as yourselves and regard the Rabbinic codifiers and discoursers as honourable men who were isolated from life.

Moses Leib Lilienblum, 1883

R. Hanina said: The Messiah will not come until a fish is sought for an invalid and cannot be procured.

Babylonian Talmud

The belief in the Messiah, the belief in the intervention of a higher power to bring about our political resurrection, and the religious assumption that we must bear patiently a punishment inflicted upon us by God, has caused us to abandon every care for our nation's liberty, for our unity and independence.

Judah Leib Pinsker, 1882

R. Jose b. Kisma said, When this gate falls down, is rebuilt, falls again, and is again rebuilt, and then falls a third time, before it can be rebuilt the Messiah will come.

Babylonian Talmud

We must determine what country is accessible to all of us, and at the same time adapted to ensure that Jews who must leave their homes go to a safe and unquestioned refuge, capable of being made productive. This piece of land might form a small territory in north America.

Judah Leib Pinsker, 1882

What is the Messiah's name? – The School of R. Shila said: His name is Shiloh, for it is written, until Shiloh come.

Babylonian Talmud

The Argentine is the answer to this question. It has room and is willing to take in 3 million Jews.

Baron Maurice de Hirsch, 1891

The School of R. Haninah maintained: The Messiah's name is Haninah, as it is written, Where I will not give you Haninah.

Babylonian Talmud

Cyprus has everything the Jews could want of a national home. It is an island, with a pleasant, healthy climate, and rich agricultural potential. Its people have their own far larger homeland in Greece, and the purchasing of land for Jewish inhabitation has already begun.

Joseph Weiss, 1893

R. Nahman said: If the Messiah is of the living today, it might be one like myself.

Babylonian Talmud

South of Jerusalem, upon a pleasant hill and served by numerous wells and foundations whose crystal waters are sweet to the taste, the olive trees grow fresh and the vintage vines turn purple beneath the ripening clusters. The hills are girded with delight and the valleys adorned with a rich embroidery of flowers. The young lambs gambol, the herds of cattle pasture and the land flows with milk and honey.

Abraham Mapu, 1851

Elke

Dunsk, 1893

To my dear brother Ephraim Tocher, I thank you for your letter which arrived here by wagon last week. We are very happy to hear from you after so long and to know that you are alive and in good health and doing so well in this Sunderland with your furniture business and your four daughters even if you have no sons and your new house and keeping a good Jew. I only hope that a good Jew in this Sunderland is the same as a good Jew here and not like in America where we hear they eat pork and smoke on the Sabbath and married women go with their own hair and other abominations. I can inform you that we are all in good health in Dunsk and following the path of God. I am glad that my little brother has been honoured with his appointment to the committee of the synagogue in this Sunderland even if the synagogue has not yet been built.

Here we have the same old synagogue that has been here a hundred years. It is not so easy to make a living in Dunsk as it seems in this Sunderland but we survive. Nahum still has the mill if most of the money he makes there does not fall into our pockets. For forty years Nahum's father and now Nahum have held this lease and one day this Haman of a tax inspector comes and tells us that the mill is outside the limits of the town and a Jew cannot hold the lease on a property that is not in the town. Nahum has found a Gentile to hold the lease but now we have to pay him also not to mention what the Haman demanded, may he live in a house with a thousand rooms and in each room have a stomach-ache. This is the way of life here, it is God's will. Last year my second son Boris had his barmitzvah, perhaps you know this from Father's letter which informed you about Israel. This barmitzvah was not like Israel's when three Rabbis kissed his head and even the country Jews walked in from the villages to hear him talk. With Boris you have to chase the words from his throat. He is a flourishing tree of a boy but no scholar. Nahum took him from school and apprenticed him to a livestock dealer. As the teacher said you cannot get gold from dross. Yossel the livestock dealer says he handles animals like a Gentile. Meyer the youngest is the bone in my throat. He has a good head on his shoulders but he uses it only for stealing apples and making mischief. The bath-house attendant caught him spying through a hole at the women last month, he said he wanted to see their beards. If you want to take one of my sons to your Sunderland take Meyer. Send a ticket for him to sail across the deep seas, maybe you can save him from growing up a thief. I am already losing my daughter Sheina. The marriage broker has found a good match for her. A good Jew, the family with a nice business making buttons. I must not complain that he lives in Riga. What is important is that Sheina has a good husband. Let no one say I am giving my daughter to the first match the broker proposed as our parents did with me. I am not complaining. Nahum is a good Jew and time has mellowed him. At least I will be able to visit Sheina on the train. You write about Israel's glorious scholarship. Do not think we have not suffered for this education. Even before his barmitzvah I had to say goodbye to the boy whose tears I calmed when he fell down and hurt his knee with plum jam and whose blood I stopped with cobwebs. All these years he has come home only once or twice a year for the High Holy Days and Passover and even then my skin shivers every time he has to travel along these roads where the bandits are murderers and the policemen are bandits, may God wipe out the memory of those villains who would beat a defenceless boy within an inch of his life. It breaks my heart to think of him taking his Sabbath meal with a strange family, eating stale bread for his supper on weekday nights and sleeping on a hard board. I send you my thanks for considering Israel for this position that might be available in this Sunderland. The Jews there must be doing well to be able to send a ticket to a boy for whom you cannot promise anything. Perhaps when you have a synagogue you would be able to promise more to some other mother's son. Here I can tell you we have marriage brokers knocking at our door to make promises every week. When Israel has his Rabbi's certificate and his blue ticket of exemption from the army we will be able to find him a beautiful marriage and a good position where he can continue his studies and take his place among the great Rabbis of Zhager and Telz and Kovno and Vilna, which they call the Jerusalem of the world today. Whatever salt they demand we will pay for this boy. I could see Boris in the army and live but if they took Israel they would have to wrap me in my burial shroud. It has been my dream since he spoke the first words of the before-meals blessing while still suckling at my breast to sit in a synagogue and hear him give a service. I can still remember his first day at school, how I cut his hair and his curls fell about his head like the autumn leaves and Nahum wrapped him in his prayer shawl and carried him out of the door. Even Mottel the good-for-nothing idler teacher could see he was blessed with a genius for a pupil and promised not to hit him on the head. They are asking more and more now for a blue ticket. One boy from Dunsk cut off his finger to save himself and they took him anyway to do everything but fire a gun. Last month Lippe the baker went to the army office and came back with his pockets empty and neither his son nor his beard, both taken from him by the soldiers' sabres. But Lippe is a fool and did not pay what Nahum has put aside. God will never allow a scholar like Israel to serve in a Gentile army where they have to work on the Sabbath and eat unclean food and spill the blood of men, maybe even his own, against all the laws of Moses. We will pay what is necessary even if we have to eat only black bread for the rest of our lives. I thank you again for your letter. It warms my heart to know you are safe and well. I hope one day we will see you and your family again in this land.

Your sister, Elke, wife of Nahum.

Deuteronomy

Minutes of the meetings of the committee of the
Villiers Street Hebrew Congregation, Sunderland

7 May, 1895. After considerable discussion, agreement was
reached to delay the decision on the most important matter of
the appointment of a Rabbi to the congregation. The letter
which had been drafted offering the position to Rabbi
Platnauer in Krottingen has been put aside and a new letter is
to be sent informing said candidate of the delay and asking for
his kind patience. Mr. Nevitt, President, expressing the opinion that a correct decision was more important than a swift
one, asked nonetheless that Mr. Tocher make all efforts to
bring his nephew to Sunderland with good speed. Mr. Tocher
replied that he had already dispatched a boat ticket and other
funds for the passage, and it was noted that these have been
paid for personally by Mr. Tocher. Mr. Nevitt concluded the
meeting by turning once again to the matter of the Synagogue
Fund, saying that while, with due regard to the kindness of

Mr. Zigmond for the use of the room in his house on Zion Street for almost three years, the rented hall on Villiers Street has been a most welcome improvement as a Place of Worship for the congregation, with the appointment of a Rabbi imminent, this premises cannot be considered more than a temporary location, and efforts to raise the money to buy or build suitable accommodation for a synagogue, house of study, school and bath-house must be redoubled. In response to this call, the members of the committee, who have already drawn deeply from their own pockets, generously promised further donations of £22 10s. Mr. Poss, Treasurer, noted that the Fund now stands at £1,217 8s. 4d.

21 May, 1895. Mr. Tocher informed the committee that he has received the welcome news that Mr. Israel Dunsky is on the way to England. It was noted that Mr. Dunsky is travelling without official papers and wishes for God's blessing on his journey were unanimously expressed. Several members of the committee recalled their own perilous experiences leaving Russia without papers. Mr. Poss described how he crossed the border hidden under the hay in a cart. Mr. Sanig remembered how he was compelled to break for the one and only time in his life the Sabbath laws by carrying his bags on the Sabbath night to evade the Russian border police. Mr. Tocher told how his wife had to put a handkerchief into their baby daughter's mouth to stop her cries as they were

led through a wood in the night to the safety of Germany. It was agreed that the decision to maintain Rabbi Platnauer's interest in the position had been wise on more than one count.

28 May, 1895. Mr. Bolchover, Secretary, reported to the committee on the matter of the Jewish Burial Ground. Gratitude was expressed to the Bishopwearmouth Burial Board on its decision to waive the £600 per acre charge and allot a piece of ground in the cemetery free of charge for the use of the Jewish community. However, the committee was dismayed that authority over this Burial Ground has been granted exclusively to the officers of the Moor Street Synagogue. It was agreed that this was a most unsatisfactory situation and that a letter should be sent immediately to the Bishopwearmouth Burial Board informing them that Sunderland has two separate Hebrew congregations and requesting in that regard that authority over the Burial Ground either be given jointly to the two congregations or the Ground divided between them. Mr. Weisgard pointed out that it was exactly this kind of high-handedness by the Moor Street Synagogue that had forced the separation and a letter of protest should also be sent to the officers of said congregation.

5 June, 1895. Mr. Tocher reported the good news that he has received a letter from Mr. Dunsky in Germany and that

Mr. Dunsky should be arriving in Sunderland next week. Mr. Bolchover, Secretary, informed the committee that the Villiers Street hall was being painted and the new seats for the honorary officers that Mr. Zigmond had donated were being installed facing the congregation, not in front of the reading desk, as the committee had agreed.

19 June, 1895. Mr. Dunsky, who has been in Sunderland almost a week, was formally introduced to the committee. He was received warmly and those members who had not yet had the opportunity to welcome him into their homes urged him to take up their invitations without delay. Mr. Nevitt, President, welcomed Mr. Dunsky, and gave him a brief outline of the history of the congregation. He described how in 1882 he and a group of Jews from Krottingen had sailed from Memel to Newcastle and after several days there had been given money by the Englisher Jews of that city to go on to Sunderland. He told how he had in good faith sought membership of the Englisher synagogue at Moor Street and how like other men of learning and good family who had occupied the front pews at home he had been relegated to the back seats. Mr. Dunsky had not yet been to the Moor Street Synagogue, Mr. Nevitt said, but he would be surprised to see there his Englisher brethren dressed in top hats, sitting in a synagogue decorated like a church, listening to a Rabbi dressed like a priest. He said that after several

years of suffering this silently he and Mr. Zigmond and later the other members of the committee had started up their own Psalm and Study Societies and how these had grown into a separate congregation which now rented its own place of worship and ran its own school. He continued by telling of the discovery that the Englisher butcher of Sunderland had been selling unporged hindquarters and kidney suet and keeping meat a week without pouring water over it, and how the congregation had in consequence appointed its own butcher to safeguard the laws of Kashrut, and how now the congregation was searching for its own Rabbi to ensure that those in the community who chose to live by all of God's laws could do so. Mr. Dunsky listened to this with great interest and expressed his gratitude for his welcome to Sunderland.

26 June, 1895. It was reported that all members of the committee have now individually met Mr. Dunsky and questioned him. Mr. Zigmond expressed the opinion that Mr. Dunsky is rather young, but Mr. Tocher replied that this is a new country and a young Rabbi will help to keep our children in the faith. Mr. Nevitt, President, asked if all members had read the letters of the Rabbis of Telz and Zhager and it was noted that all had and it was agreed that Mr. Dunsky's credentials were most impressive. Mr. Heilpern recounted how on Mr. Dunsky's visit to his house

for supper he had tried an old trick from home and put a pin through the Bible and asked Mr. Dunsky to tell him what word it pierced on pages of his, Mr. Heilpern's, choice and he reported that Mr. Dunsky had replied correctly each time. Mr. Zigmond then expressed his concern that Mr. Dunsky was not married, but Mr. Tocher said that he had plans for this also. Mr. Tocher then informed the committee that he was pledging £50 to the Synagogue Fund, for which generosity the other members expressed their gratitude and upon encouragement from Mr. Nevitt a further £8. 5s. was pledged. It was agreed that as soon as the matter of the Rabbi is resolved all efforts will be turned to the Synagogue Fund.

2 July, 1895. The committee met for the great purpose of choosing a Rabbi and after long discussions the members voted nine to one to appoint Mr. Dunsky. Mr. Nevitt, President, thanked the members for their efforts and expressed his confidence that a correct decision had been made and that Mr. Dunsky would make a fine leader of the congregation. He invited Mr. Tocher to have the honour of conveying the committee's decision to Mr. Dunsky and expressed the gratitude of the entire congregation for Mr. Tocher's efforts in bringing his nephew to Sunderland and persuading the committee of his qualities. Mr. Nevitt, who announced at the beginning of the year that this would be

his last as President, expressed his hope that Mr. Tocher would stand to be elected in his place. Mr. Tocher thanked Mr. Nevitt deeply for his most generous words and said that while he did not think any man in Sunderland could replace Mr. Nevitt, he would not shrink from any challenge that would serve the Jews of this town. He recalled how when he had arrived in Sunderland he had lived with his family in one room and worked as a carpenter for three years until he had been able to start his own workshop and build up his own furniture business. He said that what could be done with a business could be done with a community, and appointing a learned Rabbi such as Mr. Dunsky was merely the first step in making Sunderland a leading centre of Jewry in England. The committee agreed that due to his youth and inexperience Mr. Dunsky would be offered a per annum of 100 guineas rather than the 125 guineas that had been agreed for Rabbi Platnauer, who has already served a congregation and has a family.

4 July, 1895. An extraordinary general meeting was called to convey the shocking news to the committee that Mr. Dunsky had turned down the position of Rabbi of the congregation. Mr. Nevitt, President, expressed his dismay at this turn of events and questioned Mr. Tocher as to the cause of Mr. Dunsky's decision. Mr. Tocher pleaded his own bewilderment and reported that he had demanded an explanation

from Mr. Dunsky several times but that Mr. Dunsky had been unable to give any good reason. Mr. Tocher said the only explanation he could offer was that Mr. Dunsky was suffering from some illness he had caught on his journey which was affecting his mind. He said he had conveyed this opinion to Mr. Dunsky and offered to send for a doctor to examine him but Mr. Dunsky had taken offense at this and packed his bags and left his house. Mr. Tocher pleaded with the committee to accept his assurances that he had done nothing to make his nephew behave in this manner. He told the committee that if Mr. Dunsky had been the Messiah he would not have been treated better in his house. He related how he had bought Mr. Dunsky a new set of clothes, how his wife had always put the choicest pieces of meat on Mr. Dunsky's plate, how he had neglected his business to introduce Mr. Dunsky to the important people of the town. He reminded the committee that he had not only paid for Mr. Dunsky's passage to England but had sent money to his parents to pay the 300 ruble fine for his evasion of military duties. He begged the committee to know that he had even hoped that Mr. Dunsky would become his own son. He said in two or three years his daughter Rachel would have been old enough to have made a fine Rabbi's wife and that when Mr. Dunsky had expressed his doubts he had told him about these hopes but they had not swayed Mr. Dunsky in the slightest. The other members of the committee recalled how they had also given Mr. Dunsky the greatest hospitality and agreed that the position they had offered him was one that any young man in his situation would welcome and that Mr. Tocher must be right that Mr. Dunsky was suffering from some illness of the mind. Mr. Zigmond said that he had thought from the start that there was something wrong with Mr. Dunsky but that no one had listened to him. Concern was expressed that Mr. Dunsky should be seen as soon as possible by a doctor but Mr. Tocher said this was not possible as Mr. Dunsky had left his house and seemed to have disappeared from Sunderland. The last Mr. Dunsky had been seen was walking away from Mr. Tocher's house in the opposite direction from the railway station. It was agreed that if Mr. Dunsky had not been found and seen by a doctor within three days a letter would be urgently dispatched to Rabbi Platnauer in Krottingen offering him the position.

Exodus

Northern England, 1895

Happen he was one of them Ishmaelite hawkers.

*

I was up to my elbows in washing when the foreigner knocked
on the door. A glass of water he wanted, once I made out his
queer way of talking. We don't have glasses but I'll fetch you
a mug, I told him. Sit on that piece of wood. He looked
nervous towards the hog but I told him there was nowt to be
afeard on, he's one of the family, till the day Tommy cuts his
throat for bacon. He was right droothy. I brought him another
mug. Bide for a while, I told him, but he didn't.

*

Out ratting I was in the fields aback the slag heaps. That's
the best time for varmint, first thing. A penny a dozen tails

they fetch. If I catch a big'un I cut the tail in half and say I got two. He looked like he'd slept the night on the slag. He was doing the queerest things, winding a piece of leather round his head and ducking and moaning like he was dying. When he was finished he lit up a gasper, his leathers still round his head. I stopped with him for a bit. Lids, he kept saying. I vant lids. Vich vay lids. Gaumless, I reckon he was. When I saw I wasn't getting any of his gasper I left him there. I had rats to catch and school to gan to.

*

It was out of charity I let him stay the state he was in. Where've you come from? I said. Russia, he said. Looks like it too, I said, and never a bath along the way. Well you're the wrong country, I said, I can't lodge you.

I have money, he said.

I don't care what you've got, I told him. No Jews and no Russians neither, that's the rules.

That's when he showed me his purse and I felt a little charity inside me.

It'll be a bob for the bed and sixpence for breakfast, I said, and if any of the others tells you he's paying less he's lying. No drinking, mind, this house is teetotal. I know what you foreigners are like. And no spitting on the floor. There's spittoons if you've the need.

He gave me the one and sixpence on the spot. I asked him

if he was staying in Durham, but he said he was passing through on his way south. I've never yet been further that way than Spennymoor myself.

You can wash out back, I told him, I've just done the laundry and I don't want the sheets all hackied.

Up with the larks he was. I came down and he was waiting for his breakfast. Took his tea without milk and didn't want his bacon so I gave him extra egg and toast.

*

I was walking past Snaith's when I heard the commotion. Shouting and blathering inside the shop. What's all this then? I said when I got through the crowd.

Snaith was red in the face behind his counter and jabbing his finger at the foreign gentleman.

He's one of them Christ-killers, Snaith said. He admitted as much.

I am not kill anyone, the foreign gentleman started shouting. From the look in his eyes I'll wager he was thinking he was the one going to be killed.

It's all right, I told him, I'm a policeman, though that didn't seem to calm him much.

This is a respectable shop, Snaith said. I told him I don't serve Christ-killers.

I am not kill anyone, the foreign gentleman started up again.

Of course you didn't, I told him. He's talking about Jesus Christ, the son of God. From the Bible.

He must have understood something of that for he started nodding and muttering to himself.

Now, I said to Snaith, if I remember rightly our Lord was put on the cross some time ago and none of the perpetrators are still at large.

I'm not serving him, Snaith said.

If you don't hold your tongue I'll have you in for making false accusations. That quieted him. Now, I said to the foreign gentleman, what are you wanting?

Bread and cigarettes it was.

You've got money? I asked him.

He showed me the coins in his hand.

Serve the man then, I told Snaith, and we can all get on with our day.

He wasn't staying in Ferryhill, the foreign gentleman. He was passing through. I showed him the road to Darlington and watched him take it.

*

Near kicked me on the floor, he did. Started shouting I was thieving his money. What's up, I asked him. I was just trying to get in without waking you. It's my bed, he said. I paid money. So did I and all, I told him. A tanner to share a bed. It's a shilling if you want to kip on your own. I pay shilling, he said. Well that's most like because you're foreign, I told him. Now budge up and let us both get some sleep. I've got to be at the ironworks in seven hour. I prefer sleeping on my own myself, unless it's with a lass of course. But a tanner's a tanner and I like a nip now and then. I'll hand it to him, though, he stood up to the landlord in the morning and got his sixpence back.

*

You make friends easy on the road. Make them easy and lose them easy. The Hebrew I met outside Darlington.

You're lucky you ran into Silk John Clegg, I told him. I'm a friend of Hebrews. There's some as don't like them, calls them dirty, says they've got queer ways, that they spoil the trade by undercutting the English traveller. That doesn't worry me. I've got my speciality. Silks and satins. They know me where I go and won't buy silks and satins from anyone but Silk John.

I am not pedlar, he said.

I can see that, I told him. But you're on the road nonetheless.

I am going to Leeds, he said.

You go where you like, I told him. That's the beauty of the road. I go south in the winter and north in the summer like the birds. I've sold beads, buttons, buckles, brushes, braces and bodkins in my time but now I'm settled on silks and satins. Easy on the back, heavy on the pocket. It's good to have a speciality. One fellow I knew dealt only in human hair. Not strictly a mugger. Bought hair on the road and sold it to a wig-maker. He'd cut the tresses from your head if you turned your back. I never went to sleep in his company.

We walked together for half a week, me and that Hebrew. His English wasn't so clever but he was quick to learn. Wrote words down in his own letters and studied them at night. I taught him some myself. Told him about the road, too. Where to sleep and where not. Which farms are like to give a cup of tea and a piece of cake. Who to watch out for. Keep your feet clean and walk barefoot if there's grass, I told him, though he wouldn't take off his boots, even at night. Ready to run, I suppose.

There's wisdom in that, I told him. I've got nothing against your sort myself but there's some Christians would rather you were back in Jerusalem.

Some Jews also, he said.

You wouldn't know it from the number coming to this country, I told him.

It wasn't Jerusalem, but when I first met him I had in mind the place we were making for that Friday. You should have seen his face when I led him into the inn at the cross-roads and he set eyes on his brethren. The Hebrew supper club, I told him. Didn't I say you were lucky to run into me?

I sat with my beer and pie and listened to them jabbering away. Men of the road all of them except him, they meet every Friday to celebrate the Hebrew Sabbath. One of them comes in the morning to pluck a chicken and prepare it right. They've even got their own pans and bowls they chalk with Jewish writing so as no one else can use them and dirty them up without their knowing.

When the food came he passed me a plate of chicken and vegetables.

I've got my pie, I told him, but he wouldn't take no for an answer.

I couldn't understand a word they were saying but there's more than one way of knowing what people are talking about. After they'd finished eating and sung all their songs, one old fellow among them started telling the others how he had been robbed. He practically acted out the deed, showing round his empty bag and pulling at his white beard. That was when my lad took out his set of the leather straps and little boxes they pray with and gave them to the old fellow. You'd have thought there was gold in the box the way the old Hebrew kept kissing him and thanking him and weeping.

The next day when we were walking I asked him why he'd given them away. He said they were spare, but that wasn't the truth. I'd had a look in his bag one night when he was sleeping. There was only one set of them in there.

We parted the next afternoon. He was going south, I was heading west into the Dales. I always go that way the last of summer. I've customers expecting me.

*

We were only skylarking him. Asking for water. Whoever thought of walking into a pub and not wanting something to warm your heart. Here's some water for you, Tom Bolland told him. A nice pint of Yorkshire water. All grateful he were until he took a mouthful, spat it out down his coat. There weren't any harm done, it didn't mess him up any more than he already was. Old Fred gave him his water in the end. He sat there dipping his dry bread in it.

*

I was keeping half an eye on the stranger, we don't get many of his sort round here, when one of them lads from over the hill came in asking for cigarettes for his father. I told the little bugger to clear off. That's when I saw the stranger's eye on me. He asked why I hadn't sold the boy the cigarettes as he'd said they were for his father. I told him not to believe everything people tell him, specially not lads like that. He said the boy would just go to another shop and buy them. I told him I couldn't stop that but I wasn't selling them to him, it was against my principles. The way he looked at me you'd have thought he was the Englishman and I was the foreigner.

*

I let him sleep in the barn, seeing as it were coming on. Don't disturb the beasts, mind, I told him. He didn't need to tell me where he was going. I knew the first sight I had of him. When you wake get going and keep straight, I told him. It's only a matter of half-a-dozen mile.

1 Chronicles

From Leeds Evening Chronicle, *1898*

New Jerusalem (as some local joker has dubbed the Leylands) is an obscure part of the city, situated on a low-level, and confined between North Street, Skinner Lane and Lady Lane. It comprises a dirty, shabby slum of cobbled streets, crowded with back-to-back houses, black with age and a city atmosphere thickened by fishy odours. The legends at the corners – 'Myrtle Street,' 'Tulip Terrace,' 'Hope Street' – are a pathetic appeal to the imagination which turns giddy at the brazen suggestion. Truly the builders of this dismal quarter possessed an elaborate sense of humour.

New Jerusalem, as the name denotes, is the district where the children of Israel most do congregate. Where a mere fifteen years ago native traders reaped their necessarily marginal profits, the Jewish butcher, baker and candlestick maker now hold dominion. Ann Carr's old chapel on Regent

Street, latterly a Roman Catholic place of worship, is now transformed into a synagogue or Jewish reading room, and similar conversions have been made by many another institution. I believe some of the public houses are still in the hands of 'Christians', the distinguishing term by which natives are generally classified, but they are islands in a sea of Israel. Of the houses three-fourths are inhabited by the Jews, who continue to multiply by process both of immigration and of breeding with the unfailing fecundity of their race.

If Regent Street still has some residue of 'Christian' influence, then to step onto Hope Street or Byron Street is to be transported as if by the artistic skills of one of our great novelists into the Orient. Stalls at every corner and available space are piled high with garlic sausages and smoked fish while vendors dip encrusted arms into barrels of herring and pickled cabbage. Foreign names and advertisements adorn every shop, whose proprietors stand at the open doors clutching at the sleeves of each passer-by and beseeching him to buy some wonderful product which is invariably cheap and unpleasant. The noise is constant and the smell must be experienced to be believed. As for those who make up the throng, every man has the beard and eagle-nosed visage of a Biblical patriarch, though their carriage is not proud and upright, but stooped and shambling, their eyes forever glancing sideways; while the women, a few dark-eyed beauties apart, are in the main plump, swarthy and bewigged.

How the Jews have managed to take over this quarter so rapidly and completely is due simply to their great desire to fraternize and their willingness to pay heavily for this privilege. Those natives who remain bemoan that the Jews offer every inducement to the owners of property to raise the rents of the various rookeries. Back-to-back cottages of one bedroom, a living room and no cellar (save for coals), which were formerly rented at 2s. 9d. per week, have by means of this competition gradually increased to 4s. per week. In order to have first claim on a house, the Jews will even go to the lengths of paying an entrance fee, sometimes as much as 30s. being paid down for the key of a tenement.

'But,' I remarked to an informant, 'how do they afford to pay such rents!'

'Oh,' the reply was, 'they take in lodgers and sometimes a couple of families occupy one house.'

'In a house of one bedroom?'

'Yes, they manage right enough.'

A similar process has enabled the Hebrews to take over the economy of the quarter. Tailoring, and to a lesser extent slipper-making, are the dominant trades of this part of the city and they have fallen into the hands of the Jews, not in this case from a willingness to pay more, but from a readiness to take less in wages and work longer hours than their English counterparts. It is not always acknowledged that the sweating industry famous from London to New York was invented here in Leeds. A Jew named Friend, realizing that half the task of making a suit is wasted on the expense of a skilled tailor, began to hire less skilled, and so cheaper, workers to complete labours such as buttonholing and sewing the linings. Able, thus, to offer lower rates than his competitors to the whole-sale firm, and so receiving more orders than he could complete in his factory, he passed on work to employees, and they in turn rented machines and hired men to work in their own homes, becoming the so-called 'bedroom masters' whose machines hum in almost every Leylands house.

Among any people other than Jews, this system would have been unlikely to flourish, for Englishmen like to be sure of their wages, to work certain and reasonable hours and are not every one of them desperate to swap their position as artisan for that of master. But the Jew, to a man, is willing to under-cut another man's wage to get his job, to work any length of hours, and has no interest in unionization, for that would only limit his flexibility to move on and upwards. There is no race on earth possessed of such a trading instinct. There are more traders and employers among the Jews, to the acre, than there are amongst the Gentiles to the mile. As soon as the Jewish workman masters the rudiments of the trade, he looks around for 'greeners' to employ and sets up business on 'his own hook'. He will compete with his or any other fellows to the death for orders. He has no scruples as to race, creed or friendship. Money is his only guardian and friend.

It must, in fairness, be admitted that the temper of the Leylands is improved this last decade or two, for in 'Christian' days the character of the district was distinctly rough and ready, and whatever else they are, the Jews are not in the main part ruffians and drunkards. But what has been gained in temper has been lost in appearance. In conversation with a landlord, a surgeon of some renown in the city, I was given this illuminating portrait: 'I would go into a house twenty years ago and find a little palace, as comfortable as any man would want, with clean floors and blinds on the windows and nicely furnished. But if I go into that same house tomorrow I should find the floors dirty, the windows cracked and broken, the fireplaces stopped up, rags and other rubbish piled in the corners and out in the yard.'

To the Hebrew, dirt and discomfort seem of no concern. To live in the Leylands he will keep a family of five or six in one room for the price of two rooms a few hundred yards away, and rent out a bed in that room to a lodger for another shilling a week. Seldom is either his person or his home cleaned and refuse is simply thrown out into the streets. With fish being his staple diet, much of this consists of fishbones and heads, and the odour emanating cannot be described. Rats abound and the hazard to health must be perilous. One can only hope that an epidemic does not soon break out here, one which might spread beyond the limits of the ghetto.

Of the country that has given them refuge, the Jews in the Leylands seem to know nothing and have no interest. They arrive at Hull, or some other port, and come directly to the ghetto and many do not leave it again. They do not speak English and make no attempt to avail themselves of the cultural richness of which this city is proud. Other than money-making and gambling, the weakness of the Jews, the only activities are Saturday afternoon strolls in the North Street Recreation Ground, universally known among Christians as Sheeney Park, and attendance of a few societies, such as the Leeds Hebrew Literary Society. This latter is not as grand as it sounds, being a weekly gathering in whatever cellar or kitchen is available of, perhaps, a dozen out of the more than 10 thousand Jews in Leeds to read from Hebrew literature and practise the speaking of Hebrew (remembering the native tongue of the Jews is not this ancient language but the bastardized German called Yiddish), in preparation for the forlorn and farfetched dream, held by a small minority of Hebrews, of establishing a Jewish home again in that desolate corner of the Turkish Empire which their Biblical forefathers long ago habited.

Only in one place does one see the Jews conjoining in any way with England and that is in the schools, which are like rays of light in the darkness. The Gower Street School, universally known as the Leylands, is attended by 536 children of which 529 are Jewish. Walking through the corridors one sees disciplined lines of Jewish children in white pinafores and Eton collars, and if one puts one's head round the door here are Jewish boys and girls performing feats of mental gymnastics or reciting haunting lines from Tennyson's 'In Memoriam'. It is a strange thing to see and hear and where it will lead is hard to say. We take the Jewish children, tender chicks with all the sadness of centuries in their appearance. We teach them our language, banish the shadows from their lives, impart to them the shining faces of our children, that morning look to which Shakespeare refers. Then we develop the germ of cleverness within them, the germ which is to be found in all the children of Israel, and fit them to employ against our own people the unparalleled gifts of industry with which they have been endowed.

What that will mean in the long term for this country must trouble finer minds than mine. For this city, in the short term, one must only hope that a conflagration is not soon upon us, whether plague or civil disturbance, for the resentment over housing and employment is already such that a spark would set aflame an anti-foreign riot. Already the city is overloaded with the aliens; yet more are arriving every day. One has only to go down to the railway station to see them coming off the train in their ragged clothes, clinging to their pathetic parcels, and demanding to be taken to the Leylands.

Bella

Leeds, 1900

show him the piece of paper with Mordecai's and Gittel's address written on it in English which she had kept safe against her breast all the way from home but he would not even look at it and set off pushing his cart down the platform. We thought perhaps he was stealing us and our bags and Pearl was ready to scratch out his eyes as Mother instructed but it was all we could do to keep him in sight. We pushed through the crowds after him and came out onto a great wide road full of people and vehicles with grand shops and buildings along either side. Some of the buildings were like palaces and I wondered with Gittel writing about the house made of brick on three storeys and Mordecai doing so well whether perhaps one of these might be our new home, but the cart man kept on going until eventually he turned off the wide road onto a narrower one and from there to one narrower still until I realized the people around us were dressed familiarly and speaking Yiddish. How the cart man knew without asking that we were Jews or that this was our destination I do not know, but now we were able to ask for this house and were soon directed here. I was so relieved when I saw Gittel I could not say a word and Gittel asked Pearl what Mother was doing sending a dumb girl to Leeds, how were they going to find a husband for a girl without a dowry or a voice. England it seems has not changed our sister. I found my voice eventually to greet her and the boys and Mordecai when they came home. Samuel and Benjamin I hardly recognized. They have grown as with yeast these past three years. In their school clothes they look like little princes, and hardly Jews, and indeed their school is an English one, and all their lessons are in English, though I am glad to write they are learning Hebrew at home. We washed in hot water for the first time in weeks and last night, our bellies swollen with hot food, we slept on feather beds on a fold-out cot Mordecai bought specially for us. We are glad to be here and curious to see what our new lives will be.

29 May. Pearl and I went with Gittel this morning to take the boys to school. Some children run on their own, but Gittel will not let Samuel and Benjamin as Gentile boys throw stones at them and steal their caps. We saw some this morning, they did not throw anything, but they made faces

and called names. I am still growing used to the idea that Samuel and Benjamin go to an English school. Most of the children are Jews but all the lessons are in English and even when they are home Samuel and Benjamin sometimes speak English to each other. What kind of Jews they will grow up to be I do not know, but at least they have Hebrew lessons here every Sunday afternoon. School does not cost anything but uniforms and books must be paid for and even the boxes to keep their pencils in cost sixpence each. It is not cheap to live here we are learning. The rent of a good house at home would not even get you a pigsty here, Gittel says. The house is tall but very thin and dark, other houses lean against it on all sides except the front. Three rooms are ours, two others are rented by others. Pearl and I sleep in the kitchen which is buried half underground. Through the high small window you can watch legs and shoes going past. None of the houses have gardens, I do not think we have seen a blade of grass since we came here, and every potato or onion or egg you want to eat you have to pay for, though there is nothing you can buy at home that you cannot get here. That is Mordecai's business. We went with Gittel to the market yesterday. That there could be so many Jews and every one of them a stranger is hard to believe. I keep looking for familiar faces or thinking I hear a familiar voice but when I turn round it is only more strangers. Most of them are men, which pleases Pearl. She is as eager to be married as

71

Mordecai and Gittel are to see her so. Apparently they already have a suitor for her, a good Jew from a good enough family. He came here some years ago with nothing but he has built up a business and is willing to take a wife without a dowry. He will be invited as soon as we have got rid of the lice who journeyed without tickets in our hair. We discovered them at the bath-house and we smell like lamps as Gittel has scrubbed our heads raw with kerosene. She does not want us to cut our hair and look like married women even before Pearl has met her suitor.

10 June. It is Sunday afternoon and Mordecai and Gittel have lain down for a sleep. The boys' Hebrew teacher has arrived and is giving them their lesson at the kitchen table. Pearl is at the stove rolling dough for biscuits and I am curled up here in the corner with my little book, listening to the boys chanting their lesson. All would be perfect if not for Pearl's suitor, though I do not think Reb Simcha was as bad as Pearl complained. It is true he was older than we had expected, with more white hairs in his beard than black, and a widower, which Mordecai had not told us, but I think it was unfair of Pearl to say the grave was the only place his wife could have escaped his chattering. I thought what he said was quite interesting. He told us all about his business, he has a factory making coats and employs a dozen people. Tailoring here is not like at home where one man makes a

whole suit, it is divided up in a very scientific and modern way which benefits everyone, the buyer who gets his coat cheaper, the Jews who come to Leeds who can get work, and the employer like Reb Simcha who can make a little profit. He shares the same opinion with Mordecai of the Socialists and Unionists who think workers should be paid even when they are lazing about doing nothing. Reb Simcha whispered in Mordecai's ear that he was in favour of the match but when he had gone Mordecai told Pearl this, she snorted as she does and said she would not marry someone else's aged leftovers. Gittel told Pearl that she was not so young herself at eighteen and at her age Gittel was married with Samuel already swelling her belly. If it had not been the Sabbath I think there would have been more shouting than there was, as it is clouds hang over this house and Pearl has been baking as if possessed. While I have been writing this, the biscuits have come out of the oven and I think I am going to put down my pen and try one before the boys and the Hebrew teacher eat them all.

26 June. Walking the boys to school today I must admit I felt a little jealous watching the girls in their school dresses with their books under their arms. The oldest of them are not much younger than me. If I had come a few years ago I would be going to school and learning about the kings and queens of England and mathematics and reading English

poetry. I have begged to be allowed to go to the free English classes for adults at the school in the evening which the Hebrew teacher told us about. It turns out that Mordecai went to them when they first came here, but Gittel says it is one thing for the cock another for the hen. That was for his business and what do we need to speak English unless we are planning to marry an Englishman. Pearl of course does not care, she is interested only in finding her husband before she is an old maid and unmarriageable which she says she will be if she is not wed before she is twenty. Her eyes are on the next Sabbath when her new suitor is coming to supper. Mordecai has promised that he is young and has never been married. His business is even better than Reb Simcha's, he makes uniforms for the soldiers fighting in the war against the Boers in Africa which Samuel and Benjamin are always talking about and playing at with the other boys in the street. He is learned also, Mordecai said, for he studied Talmud for several years at home. I am hoping that this time we will have a match.

3 July. I am lying on our cot while Pearl is brushing her hair before we go to sleep. The Sabbath ended only an hour ago. Pearl's new suitor is coming again tomorrow and we are all praying that she will grow to like him as he seems to like her. She is certainly not so against Reb Hayyim as she was Reb Simcha even if he is rather thin and only picked at the Sabbath feast we had prepared so beautifully and Pearl

thinks that men should be solid and have good appetites. I told her perhaps he ate so little because he was nervous about meeting her and is thin because without a woman to look after him he has neglected his health and eating and needs only some feeding up. I was nervous that he would talk as much as Reb Simcha but in fact it was quite the opposite, he was very considered, and instead of talking showed his feelings by smiling at Pearl.

11 July. I am so happy. We are going to the theatre, Reb Hayyim has invited Pearl and me to see a play, he came this afternoon and brought with him three tickets to the Yiddish King Lear in two weeks time. It is a play from London, the players are the Russian Jewish Operatic Company, they are famous all over England. I was worried Pearl would reject Reb Hayyim's offer as the afternoon had not been going so well, I was so relieved when she accepted that I wanted to kiss everyone, even Reb Hayyim. Pearl spent the whole morning baking biscuits and cakes, not in anger this time but for Reb Hayyim, but even knowing she had made them herself he still only picked at a few crumbs like a bird. I could see Pearl's expression growing blacker and blacker but he obviously could not for he kept smiling at her with his thin face. The day was only rescued by his invitation and the arrival of the boys and the Hebrew teacher who had finished their lesson. If only Reb Hayyim could have eaten half as many

biscuits and been half as complimentary to Pearl as them. After Reb Hayyim went the Hebrew teacher said it was a pity we were not going to the English King Lear which he said is better than the Yiddish one though Pearl told him not for us, as we would not be able to understand it. When she said this he went red as a beet and was soon gone as well.

13 July. This house is in great excitement, even though our visit to the theatre is still a week and a half away. I have not seen Gittel looking so happy and Mordecai keeps talking about what a good business Reb Hayyim has and how the war looks like it will go on for years. I think they are already seeing Pearl and Reb Hayyim under the wedding canopy, though she says if they think that accepting an invitation to the theatre is the same as accepting an invitation to marriage then they are mistaken as if that is the case then Reb Hayyim must be marrying me as well as I have also accepted his invitation. Gittel has given Pearl a dress which no longer fits her and Pearl is going to alter it and also ungreen it as she says with some lace and lowering the neck and she is going to put bows on one of Gittel's hats, as we have seen some other ungreened Jewish girls wearing. I have only my dress from home but I will do with it what I can.

15 July. We have been shopping for everything we need to alter our dresses. I got a satin bow I am going to put on the

front. When we were out we met the Hebrew teacher. It was his lunch break from work. He is only a part-time Hebrew teacher it turns out. His main job is as a presser in a shop like Reb Simcha's, pressing coats and trousers made in the modern method. He seemed very happy to see us and apologized for what he said about the Yiddish King Lear, though even apologizing made him go a little red in the face again. Pearl was very gracious to him, if she could only be so gracious to her suitors she would perhaps already have a marriage contract. He is not at all like Hebrew teachers at home. He is not old, he does not have a beard and he wears a tie, though wearing a tie does not mean you are a heretic here and in Leeds you have to get used to seeing men's chins. Pearl's dress I think will be very beautiful and ungreen.

28 July. I have fallen in love with the theatre. It was the most wonderful evening of my life. I wept and wept and most of the time I did not know whether I was crying from happiness or sadness at the tragedy of the play. We put on our altered dresses, Pearl looked like a princess, and Reb Hayyim came to collect us in a carriage with a box of chocolates for Pearl. The theatre, the Albert Hall, is outside the Jewish quarter, and even the gentiles looked at us as we rode along. It was a big theatre with hundreds of seats but ours were very close to the front with such a view you could see the sweat on the faces of the players, though from the minute

the curtain opened I did not think they were players but the very people they were playing. It was not about any king or anyone called Lear, it was the story of Reb David Moscheles, a wealthy Jew from Vilna who decided to pass on his wealth to his daughters so he could live out his old age in simplicity in Jerusalem. His two older daughters were happy but his youngest Teibele begged him not to go away or give up his riches, and he grew so angry with her for disrespecting him that he disinherited her and gave everything to the other two. But when he got to Jerusalem he found the older daughters were really monsters though I could have told him that myself. They did not send him even the few rubles he had asked for to live on and he had to come back to Vilna, where they treated him even more shamefully until he was driven mad and blind and was reduced to begging for food, dressed in rags and tearing at his hair. Only with the help of his faithful friend Shammai did he manage to regain his sanity and go blindly in search of the youngest daughter, who in her own despair had determined to end her life. That was when I wept the most, and I was not the only one, though thankfully David reached Teibele in time and saved her life. On the advice of his lawyers he renounced his legacies to the older daughters and they were forced to beg for his forgiveness, which he gave them, and it turned out Teibele who had gone to university to study medicine had married a brilliant doctor, Jaffa, who restored old David's sight so everything could end happily. While we watched we ate the chocolates Reb Hayyim had bought and afterwards we had ice cream and then we drove home again in a carriage. I am very tired as we stayed out so late and Pearl and I lay awake half the night talking about the play and repeating the words.

29 July. My head is all turned around and I do not know where to start so I shall do so at the beginning. Reb Hayyim came to see Mordecai and made a formal proposal of marriage to Pearl but when Mordecai brought this to Pearl she made ashes and dirt of the offer. This was not a surprise to me as I knew how she really felt about Reb Hayyim but Gittel and Mordecai had thought she was almost already married and were very angry. Gittel said who was Pearl to turn down a proposal from such a good Jew who did not want a single penny for a dowry but Pearl said she could not marry a skeleton like Reb Hayyim who had hardly said a word to her and wouldn't eat her biscuits or even compliment her on them, let alone notice the dress she worked so hard to alter or compliment her on her looks and only grinned at her like a madman. If Pearl would not have Reb Hayyim, Mordecai said, then he would go back to Reb Simcha and see if he would renew his suit. Pearl said Reb Simcha was even worse than Reb Hayyim. If all Jewish women were like this Mordecai said no Jews would get married, no Jewish children would be born, in a few short years

there would be no Jews, Pearl would achieve the greatest desire of the Jew-haters. Gittel said she had to marry someone, she could not sit on their necks for ever. That was when Pearl said if she had to marry someone she would rather marry the Hebrew teacher than either of her suitors. Gittel wailed that Pearl would prefer a poor Hebrew teacher over two men with their own businesses but Pearl told her he is not a Hebrew teacher, he is a presser in a tailoring shop. Gittel said an ignorant tailor was even worse than a Hebrew teacher but Mordecai said the Hebrew teacher is not ignorant at all, he would not allow an ignorant man to teach his sons and the Hebrew teacher is a learned man. He said he had not thought about the Hebrew teacher as a suitor as there were men with money who wanted Pearl, but if she didn't care about money maybe it wasn't such a bad idea as a scholarly man like this was not to be sniffed at. Gittel said for a girl like Pearl any man with two legs and a heart that is still beating was not to be sniffed at.

31 July. The Hebrew teacher has been invited for the Sabbath supper.

5 August. Pearl is baking again, for soon Reb Israel will be here to give the boys their lesson. The house is happy for it seems that Pearl really does like Reb Israel and he likes her. Gittel has even started turning her mind to my future, this

morning she said that if I am going to be as picky as Pearl maybe they should start looking for a suitor for me sooner rather than later. If they could find me one like Reb Israel I would not be unhappy. There is something thoughtful in his face that I like and I think Pearl likes too. When you ask him a question he listens gravely and considers before he talks and then answers the whole question until it is all answered, though that does not mean he is like Reb Simcha who I think in truth liked only to listen to his own voice. He does not smile much but when he does smile his face changes. He has a neat moustache on his lip, brown in colour, like his hair which is thick and curly but cut quite short, and he wears spectacles. It is a good face and honest I think, like I hope his character. He has relatives in another town in England but he has not seen them for some years. When he first came to England he walked from that town to Leeds, which he seemed to be quite proud of doing though Mordecai said there was a train he could have taken. When he came to Leeds there was a shortage of work and it took him some time before he became an underpresser and finally a presser in tailoring shops. He teaches Hebrew to make a little extra money and also because he believes Jews should know Hebrew as he is one of these Lovers of Zion we have heard about. He helped to found a society which meets every week to speak Hebrew and read and discuss Hebrew writing. Mordecai was not very impressed with this and said this whole business of a Jewish homeland is foolish dreaming, the only people who go to Palestine are religious Jews and lunatics and old men who want to die there like in the Yiddish King Lear. He asked Reb Israel if he had considered starting his own shop here and if it was a matter of money he was sure something could be arranged. He said that Reb Israel should come to talk to him another time as this was not really a subject for the Sabbath evening and for now he should enjoy his food, which he did it must be said, he is definitely solid and a good eater.

5 August. Evening. Pearl and I and Reb Israel have been for a wonderful walk in the park. After Reb Israel had drunk his tea and eaten almost a whole plate of Pearl's biscuits, he suggested we go as it was such a fine afternoon and he needed to walk off the biscuits. I was very happy to walk among grass and trees again and hear the singing of birds other than the pigeons that cluck on the window-sills and cover them in their droppings. I was careful to hang back a little and let Pearl and Reb Israel walk on ahead, though not so far that I could not hear what they were saying. They talked a little about home and found that they had swimming in common. Reb Israel apparently was a strong swimmer as a boy and could swim across the great river that ran by his town, while Pearl told him how we would swim in our nightgowns. Then Pearl asked him if he had any plans to

start up his own shop as Mordecai had suggested. Reb Israel said he did not think so as the way the shops work it is hard for the boss not to exploit his workers. Pearl said that sounded like Socialist and Unionist talk and Reb Israel said if it did it was because he had worked in the shops for five years and knew what it was like, it was not so bad for him as he was not married and had his teaching as well but for men with families it could be hard to make ends meet, especially in the slack time when they were not paid. We walked in silence after that and I think Reb Israel must have realized he had been too serious for a suitor, for the next thing he said was about a real Socialist presser he knew who used to put Socialist leaflets into the pockets of every coat he pressed and when he was fired for doing this and became a baker he put the leaflets into every loaf of bread he baked, and we all laughed at this, I also, and they turned round in surprise, for I think they had forgotten I was there. We came home then as Reb Israel had to hurry off to do his Lover of Zion work. On Sunday nights he goes around collecting money for the Jewish homeland, and signing up members for his society.

7 August. We have been to see Reb Israel at his shop. Pearl decided we should surprise him with lunch today and she made him a little package of bread and cheese and sour cucumber and some of her leftover biscuits and we walked

down to Hope Street where his shop is. I thought we should wait outside for Reb Israel to come out, but she wanted to see where he worked so we walked up the stairs and through the open door of the shop. It was very hot and steamy inside and we did not see Reb Israel at first for he was standing in a cloud of steam stripped to his vest. His skin was red with the heat, sweat was dripping from his face, he was lifting his big pressing iron and slamming it down on the coat. He was surprised to see us and hurried to put on his shirt and come over to us. He asked the boss if he could go down early for his lunch-hour as time had not yet been called and though the boss grumbled about it he let him. We walked back down and sat on the steps in the shade. Reb Israel was very pleased with his lunch. He apologized that we had seen him as we had, but Pearl said he had nothing to apologize about as we had chosen to come. Reb Israel said it was not so bad actually, you got used to the heat and handling the pressing iron though only physically strong men could be pressers. The weaker men became machinists, he said. It might seem brutal but pressing is quite an art. You have to heat the goose, that is the pressing iron, until it is exactly hot enough, and then when you have wetted it hold it for exactly the right time against the coat or trousers you are pressing. Too little heat and the material is not pressed, too much and it is burned. His shop is not a bad one either as it is unionized and they work only from eight to eight with an hour for lunch. Pearl asked him why he could not start a shop that treated the workers well, but he said it is not only bad bosses that cause the problem but the English whole-salers who pay so little for contracts that bosses have to make their employees work long hours for low pay to make any money at all and often the bosses do not make money and go out of business and end up back as machinists or pressers. He is not really a Socialist, he said, as he is not against bosses but he would not be willing to be in their position and have to treat his workers like slaves. He showed us a book he had in his pocket which he would have sat and read during his lunch-hour if we had not come to see him. It was called Self-Help by Samuel Smiles, a famous English writer, which he was reading to improve himself as he might not want to be a boss, but that did not mean he planned to be a presser all his life. It seemed like we had been there only ten minutes but Reb Israel's lunch-time was finished and he had to go upstairs and Pearl and I walked home.

9 August. I am going to marry the first suitor Mordecai and Gittel find for me however old he is or thin or talkative. We went today to take lunch again to Reb Israel and this time we waited for him to come down and when we were sitting and he was eating his food Pearl asked him what we have been wondering, if he does not want to start his own shop

and he does not mean to be a presser, what does he mean to do, and he told us he is going to Africa. He would have gone already if it was not for the war and as soon as it is finished he is going there. His brother is going to meet him there and together they will start a new life. Africa is rich with land, gold, diamonds, opportunities. There he said a man can build a life for himself and raise a family without exploiting other men. When he said this he turned to Pearl and looked at her with such soft eyes but her eyes were not soft in turn. She looked away from him and said in her voice that I know so well that she wished him luck in Africa and hoped he would find a good wife there to raise this family, though she could not imagine what kind of woman would want to bring children into the world where they would probably be eaten by wild tigers or killed by hottentots when they could do so in Leeds, where there were brick houses and theatres, though no doubt they have theatres in Africa where they show the Hottentot King Lear which no doubt is better than the Yiddish one. Then she took my hand and dragged me away leaving poor Reb Israel sitting there with his lunch half eaten. I think the old way is better, your parents arrange everything with the marriage broker, you meet your husband on your wedding day, what will be will be.

12 August. Poor Reb Israel, I do not think any man should be spoken to the way Pearl speaks to him. She would not

even greet him when he came to give the boys their Hebrew lesson. After it was finished I gave him his glass of tea, and he looked at me uncertainly and asked in a very quiet voice whether there were by any chance any of those delicious biscuits Pearl baked so beautifully. Well Pearl, who was not even looking at us, said in a loud voice that some men do not seem to know anything about how to behave, they think it is always the woman who should be providing something sweet to eat, somebody should tell some men that other men when they have come to this house have brought with them boxes of

Pearl

Germiston, South Africa

17 November 1903

My dear sister Bella,

Your letter arrived yesterday and I was very happy to hear about you and Solly and the boys and Gittel and Mordecai and Leeds. Reading your words made the sea I travelled across to get here and the land like another sea not seem so far that I will never see you again. We are well here also, though how sometimes I do not know. At least we are not overrun with rats since I bought the cat from the kosher meat man who comes every Thursday. Eli has fallen in love with this cat and follows it everywhere. He is a beautiful solid little boy, I wish you could see him. Rosa is well too. All she wants to do is sit with her father in the store. I do not like it as the customers are such ruffians but Israel says it is good for business, these ruffians come in just to hear the little storekeeper talk, that is what they call her. Rosa loves her father and Eli loves the cat and Israel loves his Zionism, I am not sure who loves me, except my dear Bella. I wonder what you would think if you saw your sister here in this iron hut behind the iron store on this square of dust. Last month I went into Johannesburg with Israel as Boris was here to keep the store and Reisl whose husband runs the liquor store across the square agreed to watch the children for the day. I walked past the theatres and hotels and in the stores my eyes were so wide I did not know what to buy, and cursed myself on the train as Israel had not held back from spending our money at the Jewish bookseller. Johannesburg would be somewhere to live but Israel says to make a fortune there you already need a fortune, to make a new fortune you must be somewhere new like Germiston. How we are going to make a fortune selling groceries from an iron shack I do not know, though Israel says as the town grows I will see we are sitting on a gold mine here in our position on the main square. He is always hopeful and never complains, but sitting in a grocery store counting pennies and stacking tins all day is not the life for a man of his intelligence. Even then we depend on the money Boris brings in from his livestock buying. He is away half the time riding out to buy from the farms and bring the animals to sell at market. I am always glad when he comes home, if not for his conversation, there is not much of that, but I feel safer when he is here. Last month some drunken ruffians came into the store looking to have some fun with the Jews, Boris took the biggest ruffian by the arms and threw him out into the dust, the big ruffian was so amazed, no one had ever done this to him before, he told Boris he could make money fighting in Johannesburg. That is the store where little Rosa sits on the counter talking English to the customers. I am still not used to it being open on the Sabbath but half our business is on Friday nights and Saturdays after the gold diggers and railway workers get paid and if we closed on the Sabbath we would have to close the doors forever. At least I am determined to keep a kosher house and bring the children up as Jews. That is our life here at the bottom of the world. Dear Bella, please write again soon. I send my love to you and Solly.

Your sister, Pearl

28 August 1904

My dear Bella,

We are all very happy for you and Solly and will be thinking about you both when the time comes. Who knows by then we may have made some money and I can come to visit you. You must promise to send us a photograph of the happy family. I am going to send you one of us as soon as I can get Israel away from the store for an hour, as we now have a photography studio in Germiston. The world is coming to us a little. We have two pharmacies, a dentist opened a surgery last month, and there is a bicycle store which Israel is very pleased about. There are plans also to build a synagogue as we have enough Jews now, though most of them seem to think our grocery store is the synagogue the way they come to stand around talking. If they bought as much as they talked I would not mind, though Israel does not help. After he has persuaded them to buy a stamp for the Jewish homeland and pay for an olive tree to be planted there they do not have any money left for groceries. There is also a big hotel going up and a new building that will have stores underneath and offices on top, though all on the other side of town where they have built the town hall. When we came we were in the middle of the town, now it seems we have moved to the edge. Israel's plan is to buy a bicycle and deliver groceries, he says we can cover the whole town that way and double or treble our business. We are waiting for Israel's brother Meyer to decide whether he is coming here from Riga. Israel has been writing to encourage him, he says with three brothers working together they will be able to build up the business better and faster. Meyer could do the deliveries, Israel would run the store and Boris would not need to go off all the time buying his livestock. Meyer was wild when he was young but since Israel's father died and the family moved to Riga he has been working for his brother-in-law's button business and it seems he has settled down. The fever has been going around here, one Jewish child died of it, she was well one day and could not breathe the next her throat was so swollen. The doctor came and cut her neck but still she died. I do not let the children drink water after eating fruit as that brings on the fever and both are well though do not stop praying for us. Eli is a solemn little boy like his father, always asking questions and wanting to know what I cannot answer. Rosa is gentle and stoical like her mother and a good little helper. I will not watch the store unless she is there to make sure I do not give sugar when customers ask for bread or beans when they want salt. I wish I had listened to you about English lessons, I do not know what I will do when Rosa goes to school. You will be interested to hear that a new play by the same writer who wrote the Yiddish King Lear has come to the Baltic Hall in Johannesburg. It is the story of a Rabbinical student who comes home to find his father dead and his mother married to his uncle, a ghost tells him his uncle killed his father, to decide what to do he travels across Russia consulting the greatest Rabbis. I have not seen it but Reisl across the square told me about it, she says it is very entertaining. If you cannot dig gold out of the ground, selling liquor is the way to make money here. Reisl's husband takes more on a Saturday night than we do in a week, but Israel will not touch a liquor license. He says at home it was liquor from Jewish inns that gave the Gentiles the courage to make pogroms and he will not be part of anything like that here. I wish you could see how my garden looks in the sunshine, dear Bella, that at least would make you jealous of me. I do not know half of what I have planted, flowers with petals the size of your hand, colours like a rainbow, smells I do not know if they are horrible or beautiful, but whatever you throw in the dust grows if you water it. I have even planted a plum tree, a customer gave me a cutting, though I do not know why I bother for if we are still living in this iron shack when it bears enough plums to make a pot of jam they will have to bury me under it. I send you and Solly a kiss.

Your loving sister,

Pearl

3 *March 1905*

My dear Bella,

Forgive me for not writing, I have not had a moment to pick up a pen with the house so full. Boris has finally left to buy some livestock and Meyer has gone with him, so we have some peace here again. It was good to have the house filled with noise and eating. Meyer is a little rough at the edges but he has life in him and he stirred his brothers to talking and playing cards every night. Last week we had our first proper Sabbath evening since we have been here. I persuaded Israel to close the store early this once and we sat to eat as the sun went down. I made Meyer take the children out and I cleaned the house as best I could and cooked all day, we sat down and ate and the brothers sang together, I felt like a real Jewish woman again. The house seems empty now that they have gone. Eli wanders about looking for Meyer to throw him into the air or chase him under the table. Meyer said he wanted to see a little of the country before he decides what to do and Boris is going to introduce him to this woman we still have not met. All we know is that she is a Courlander, and you know what they are like. The brothers talked a lot about the business and Israel is very excited about the possibilities. The town is growing and while we are not in the best place, with three brothers and a little capital perhaps they will be able to get a new premises and expand from groceries. Who knows maybe one day Dunsky Brothers stores will be all over the Rand. Meyer's arrival has made me feel more hopeful and I have been spying on some new houses they are building on the other side of Germiston, nothing too big, but proper houses with rooves that you are not afraid will fly off when the wind blows, hot water geysers in the kitchen and a verandah to sit on in the evening and sew. With a house like this I could be happy in Africa. I send my love to you and Solly and give a kiss to little Cecily.

Your sister,

Pearl

26 January 1906

My dear Bella,

To think that Samuel is a man now. We read about his bar-mitzvah greedily, Israel was very pleased to hear about his recitation. It is a long way ahead of Eli but he has started at the Hebrew school, he goes there three days a week after English school. The house seems empty with both children gone so much of the day. I dream of having another one but I will not consider it until we move into a proper house, if we ever do. I went secretly the other day into Ginsberg's, the new grocery store on two storeys that has opened here from Johannesburg. I would shop there myself, so many shelves full of goods, everything on special offer, free delivery all over Germiston. When I came home I walked into our store and Israel was giving money to some swindler who had sold him a story. I told him if at least he charged interest on these loans we could make a little money, but of course he would never do that. Our big news is that Boris and Malka have finally set a date for next month. The wedding is in Benoni though they are building in Germiston and will carry on living in the house Boris and Meyer rent until that is ready. It is hard for Israel seeing his brothers doing so well while he still struggles to make a penny. Last week Meyer signed a second contract to supply meat to the mines. It seems to me there is enough money in this meat business for three brothers but Israel will not ask Meyer and Boris and they do not ask him to join them. It breaks my heart to see Israel getting up at dawn every day to count the six dozen rolls delivered by the bakery which he sells four for a penny while Meyer walks into an office and puts his pen to a piece of paper and makes a hundred pounds. Israel says that is not all he does, something else happens under the table, but Meyer says that is how business works everywhere whether you are in Riga or Germiston. I can just hear what Gittel would say if she read this letter, but I would not have married those suitors if they had been millionaires. I only wish we could have a little luck. Did I write to you what a swindler and a fool the barber we hired to make a little extra money and bring people into the store turned out to be? The Sunday we went over to Benoni to meet Malka's family he opened up the store and started giving shaves and haircuts, when a policeman came in to see who was Sunday trading he offered to trim his moustache for half price. That is what comes of hiring Rumanians. Do not think that he was planning to share his Sunday proceeds with us but it was Israel who had to pay his fine of five pounds which is more than we ever made from the barber business. I had better stop before you think I am complaining. I have to go and start baking for the stall I am running for the Zionist bazaar. It is going to be quite an event, as well as my Cake stall there is a Flower stall, Drapery, Socks and Ties, Arts and Fancy, Toys and others I forget. Afterwards children will sing songs and recite in Hebrew. Israel has been running around all week arranging everything. If we ever get to the Land of Israel there had better be a corner there for us. Write soon, my dear Bella. I send my love and kisses to you and Solly and Cissie.

Your sister,

Pearl

17 March 1908

My dear sister,

I have been thinking about you as I always do this time of year. I suppose you are going to Mordecai and Gittel for Passover as usual. I would give anything to be with you and see little Cissie and Lionel with my own eyes. We are going to Malka's. Israel says I should be pleased, I always complain I cannot make a proper Seder in this house and I can let Malka do all the work, though I don't know what work it will be for her with her cook-general and brand new kitchen and mahogany table and matching chairs and even the shank of lamb free from Dunsky Brothers. She hardly lifts a hand in that kitchen, God knows what she lifts in the bedroom, there is no sign of anything growing in her belly. I am taking the wine I have made, I will not let my family drink store wine, but it has not been the same cleaning the house knowing we will not be feasting here. At least we will save some money. I am thinking about putting it down on a piano. For two pounds down and a pound a month you can get a Bechstein. The children might have to live in an iron house but that does not mean they cannot learn to play the piano. Rosa has a beautiful voice and Eli is a good whistler, it would break my heart to waste their talents. We cannot really afford it but otherwise the money would only go to the Jewish bookseller or end up in the blue box for the Jewish homeland or worse. Israel has just lost five pounds he had to pay to the Gemilut Hassidim. A pedlar who used to come by here selling bits and pieces asked him to guarantee a loan to start up his own business and no-one has heard from him since. Israel had to pay up the money. It made me want to weep but you know what Israel is like, he says he would rather give money to a liar than refuse it to an honest man, though for that five pounds I could have bought all our new Passover clothes and had enough left to put down on the piano. Meyer and Boris are doing business with half the mines on the Rand now as well as the butcher's they have opened near the slaughterhouse on the other side of Germiston. Meyer has even changed his name. He is Max Dunsky now, he says it is better for business to have an English name. I tell him he should make Israel a partner. If it was not for Israel he would still be making buttons in Riga. But Israel says he would not work in such a business dipping his hands in blood all day. It was the one thing he hated in his training as a Rabbi when they had to learn the laws of slaughter and cut an animal's throat. Even so, he has been going down to Dunsky Brothers to discuss a proposition with Meyer to buy the fat from the slaughtering and use it to make soap. He says all you have to do is boil up the fat and pour it into moulds and you have soap, if Meyer will let him have the fat at a good price he can make a nice profit. Who knows, Bella, maybe this scheme will work but I am not going to send the lottery man away when he knocks at the door. The other day I went into the store and Israel was sitting with a pot of jam from the shelf dipping his finger into it. He had eaten half the pot, he said it helps with his belly troubles. Sometimes I think I have married a little boy. This year maybe I will get some plums on the tree and make my own jam. That would help his belly. Think of me on Seder night as I will be thinking of you.

Your devoted sister,

Pearl

12 October 1910

My dear Bella,

What kind of land we are living in I do not know. Last night I woke, I thought the Cossacks were jumping on our roof to drag us out and kill us. It was ice, Bella. Balls of ice the size of eggs falling from the sky. All this time I have been watching for danger wriggling on the ground or poisoning us from the water we drink or walking into the store and I did not think to worry it might fall from the sky. Thank God it was night or the children might have been killed. As it is, my garden is destroyed, the plants smashed, the fruit stripped from the plum tree. I walked outside in the morning and wept to see all my hard work ruined. It is seven years now we have been in this iron hut and I cannot see how we are going to make enough money to move. For myself I do not mind but to see Israel sitting behind the same dusty counter in that store breaks my heart. His belly has been very bad and he has been buying diet books that tell him he must not eat this or only eat that, at the moment I am cooking for him without salt. I don't know how he can eat it, the bread is dry and the meat tastes raw, and you know how much pleasure he has always got from my cooking. The other day we had the worst argument we have ever had. He was reading the Jewish Chronicle from London and read out about this man he knew in Leeds or Sunderland or somewhere, he had been at theological college like Israel and secretly read all the secular books like him and become a doubter also, but he swallowed his doubts and now he has just been made Rabbi of some big town in England. Israel said maybe he should have swallowed his own doubts and taken the position in Sunderland at least he would have had a better life. It made me so angry, Bella, I told him what did he mean better, if he had taken that job he would never have met his wife, never have had his children, did he think that would be better? Maybe I told him I should have thought better when he came to me with that big box of chocolates and talked me into marrying him. What else I said I will not write down here. He stared at me and did not say a word and suddenly all the anger was gone from me and I went up to him and put my hand on his arm and told him maybe he should swallow his pride and talk to Meyer about working with him. Dunsky Brothers is expanding, they are talking about opening branches in other towns, if he talked to Meyer properly I am sure he would make him partner, we would have a little money, we could get a proper house, employ a boy or two, make a future for our children. He was very gentle also, do you remember what he was like when we first met him, so grave and serious, he was like that now. He asked me if I thought he did not consider this every day, but how could he go to work with a man like Meyer who gets every contract under the counter and treats his workers so badly. He said for Meyer the business is only about money and he does not care what happens to the men he employs, firing them without a reason, shouting at them. He said if he took any-thing from his years of studying at home it was that a man should always behave ethically. He did not give up good busi-ness opportunities in England for ethical reasons to come here and throw out his ethics. What could I say Bella? I could have married any number of rich men but I married Israel because he is a good man and a man of principle. That is my lot even if death falls from the sky on our heads. I send you my love and kiss Cissie and Lionel for me.

Your sister,

Pearl

12 May 1911

My dear Bella,

This may be the last letter I will write to you from Germiston. We are talking about leaving and starting up again in a new town where the opportunities are still fresh. Israel has met again some German brothers he knew in his first months in Johannesburg when he was selling old clothes before he came to Germiston, and with them he is making plans to start a bioscope in Bloemhof. These brothers, the Mullers, have been down there working on a diamond digging, they did not make any money, their claim was no good, but they say there are many men there on the diggings with nothing to do and there is a fortune to be made giving them some entertainment. It would be better if Israel went first but we need to sell the grocery store to have some capital so we will all have to go together. The Mullers say there is a school there, Bloemhof is not only a diggings, it is a railway town like here, we stopped there on the train from Cape Town though I do not remember. It is on the way to Kimberley, you must have heard of that from the famous diamond. I think this iron shack will be luxury compared to what we will have there but if it works out maybe it will not be long before we can afford something better. Sometimes you have to go down before you can go up. Israel says we will not waste again our chance of being in at the beginning and certainly the bioscopes here are minting money. We have three now in Germiston and we have been going to all of them so Israel can see how they work. He spends his time with his neck cricked, looking around, counting how many people are coming in at one shilling a time, trying to see the machine that makes the pictures, writing it all down on little pieces of paper. I watch the pictures and am carried away from Africa around the world. It is cheaper than getting a boat ticket. These last weeks I have seen Baffled Burglar, Motor Ride through London and Lady Candace's Jewels. Israel says once you have bought the equipment all you need is to rent the film and take the money and you will grow rich. It is the future and we are going to be in at the beginning of the future, he says. Who knows Bella maybe this time it will be true. It is not that there is anything in Germiston I love so much. I hardly see Reisl since she moved into her big house and I can live without Malka. All I care for will be coming with me, my husband, my children, my mahogany sideboard which I am not selling. Send any letters you write to Malka, she will forward them to us. I will write to you as soon as we have an address. Think of us Bella and pray for us, I do not know if God will be able to hear us from where we are going.

Your loving sister,

Pearl

Hostilities

Pretoria, 1915

Ho, you, new boy next door, Enoch or whatever your name is, what you are doing? Do you not know it is Passover? All day I have been cleaning out the homits and now you throw your sweepings into the air to blow into this house.

I can see you have got a lot to learn. Some missis will employ any fool straight from the kraal. Homits is bread that has risen. It is forbidden in the house on Passover. Even if one crumb of your homits blows onto the verandah of the house God will not bless the Passover feast.

Do you think it is my job to explain everything to you? It is not my fault your missis has employed a boy without any education. You had just better make sure you do as I say. Do you know who my baas is? You know Dunsky Brothers?

Well, that is because you are new in this town. I can tell you they are the big meat people here and my baas is the top one of these Dunsky brothers. Every day at his work he kills more cows than you probably have in your whole village.

Yes, you have seen him then. He goes to work every day on this bicycle. Now I cannot stand here all day talking to you. We have got all the Dunsky brothers and their families coming tomorrow to enjoy the Passover feast and I must go and help the missis make the kneidlach.

Ho, Enoch, it is you.

They are not eating yet. The baas is reading from the Passover book.

It belongs to Baas Max. He has just bought it. They drove over from Germiston in it. Now you can see what big people these Dunsky brothers are.

Yes, my baas is the top one. He is the oldest brother.

I think you are being cheeky. If Baas Israel wanted to buy an automobile he could buy an automobile. He rides his bicycle because he likes to ride his bicycle. If you are going to be so cheeky, I will ask you not to disturb me over the garden fence in future.

Good morning to you also, Enoch.

Yes the Passover feast is finished, but don't think that means you can throw your sweepings into the air whenever you please. I am keeping a clean house here.

I hope you are not being cheeky again, Enoch. That was

not shouting last night, it was discussing. Did I not tell you these brothers are big people. They have important things to discuss and little people like you should not be poking their noses where they do not belong.

I am reading a book, Enoch.

It is called Gem, or maybe this one is Magnet. I have got a whole pile of these Gems and Magnets.

What do you think I am, a thief? The baas found them under Master Eli's bed and told me to get rid of them and I am just having a look at them first.

I am sorry but I cannot let a young boy like you read them. These comic books are not good for young boys, they will spoil your mind. Young boys should be reading educational books like Dickens and Wells and History of Jews.

What are you doing, Enoch? Have I not told you not to throw your sweepings into the air so that they blow over here?

No it is not Passover again. It does not need to be Passover for you not to throw your sweepings into the air. The missis is sitting on the verandah trying to have some peace with her sewing, she does not want your sweepings blowing into her face when she is trying to have some peace.

It was only Baas Boris and his barren wife who came last night, that is why it was quiet. It is when Baas Max comes that they have the big discussions. He is the one with the fertile young wife and the new baby. When he comes the discussions are always very big, Miss Rosa has to get out the cards so that they can play Sixty-six and stop discussing.

That was not a box, Enoch, that was a piano.

It is not always coming in and out of the house. For your information, Enoch, it is not the same piano you have seen every time. The first time they were taking away a very old one that was no good for Miss Rosa and Master Eli to play on. The second one was the new one that the baas bought for them. The third time was when this new piano got taken away after the baas went to the judge to make the shop take it back because they had cheated him with a broken piano. This last is the good new one they have bought. Did you not hear Miss Rosa playing her music on it earlier in the evening?

Well the fact that you did not know it was music only goes to show what a shlemiel you are.

Come, Enoch, you had better leave now. They will be back from the bioscope soon.

That is the box for the Jewish homeland.

For collecting money for the Jewish homeland. These Jews are saving up to buy back their homeland, don't you even know your Bible? They have got one of these boxes in every room, you see the hole where you put in the money. They have even got one in the lavatory.

That is a different one. That is for the Jewish War Victim's Fund. The baas has been putting a lot of money into that one recently.

A cricket ball hit him there. The doctor said he might have gone blind. The baas was very angry with Master Eli for this I can tell you. He has always been telling him that sport is a waste of learning-time and good only for idlers and loafers and now look what has happened to him. Last year Master Eli almost broke his leg playing rugby and now he has almost gone blind from this cricket ball. How will he be able to study his books with this eye patch the baas does not know.

No the baas has not gone to work today. He is having trouble with his belly again. This always happens after Baas Max comes to visit. I think it must be something Baas Max brings for him to eat.

They were discussing partner and manager. That is the names they have at Dunsky Brothers. Baas Israel thinks that partner is better and Baas Max thinks manager.

I am keeping away the birds so they do not eat the plums before they are ripe and we can pick them.

You don't eat them, you make jam from them. Homemade plum jam is a very fine medicine, it can cure you of any illness you can get.

We had some trouble last night I can tell you.

Miss Rosa scratched out the eyes of the King of Russia from the front of a book.

Russia is where these people come from, don't you know anything. The baas was very shocked at what she had done, he told her that in Russia the police would come and take you away for ten years for doing a thing like this.

That is what Miss Rosa said but she did not know and you obviously do not know either that the King of Russia is a cousin of our King and do you know whether there is a law here against insulting the cousin of the King of England and South Africa? What if some policeman came into the house for some reason, to get a glass of water for someone who has fallen down in the street, and saw this book. Can you be sure Miss Rosa would not get into trouble for doing this?

He tore off the cover of this book and threw it into the fire. Miss Rosa was very upset and went straight to bed.

No she did not, but later the baas asked me to get some milk and biscuits which he took to her in her bed.

They have gone to Johannesburg to the theatre. They are staying the night in a hotel there. They are celebrating fifteen years they have been married. They have gone to see a play about an African chief who loves a beautiful white woman, though of course it is not an African who is playing him but a white man with his face painted black.

You didn't see his car because Baas Max was not here. Those discussions you heard were between the baas and the missis. It was about Master Eli's barmitzvah, that is when he becomes a man. The missis wants to have a big celebration, but the baas said what is there to celebrate that Master Eli has learned to read a few words the teacher has written out for him that he does not even properly understand. The missis is very upset; she wants to invite everybody to come here but the baas will not let her. They were still very angry this morning and the missis is not cooking anything for the baas's supper tonight. I do not know what he will eat when he comes home.

I am just having a bit of peace out here myself.

No I am not needed inside. Everything is quiet there. They are all sitting together reading. Each of them has their own book. No one is discussing anything at all.

Samuel

Achiet Le Petit, France

3 July 1917

Dear Uncle Israel, Aunt Pearl, Rosa and Eli,

Thank you so much for your parcel which arrived a couple of days ago. I hadn't had anything from home for a while so it was very welcome and I shared it with a pal who shares with me whenever he gets anything and we had a real feast. Aunt Pearl's plum jam was especially appreciated. I hope she forgives me for not writing in Yiddish but as letters have to pass the censor I am sure you will understand.

I am very pleased to hear that you are all well. It sounds like both Rosa and Eli are proper scholars at school, though you don't mention whether they are learning Hebrew. If they are not I can suggest a very good Hebrew teacher! I am glad that apart from Uncle Israel's Zionist activities you are not much affected by the war. It seems

111

from what you write that you may even be doing rather well out of it, with feeding the soldiers and everything. It is good that someone is.

By now you will probably have heard about what happened in Leeds. My family were thankfully out of it in Chapeltown but from what I heard it was pretty horrible for Aunt Bella and Uncle Solomon and the little ones especially. Their house didn't get touched but the mob went down their road shouting and waving sticks. Apparently there were hundreds if not thousands, some of them even women and girls. Dozens of shops were smashed up and looted and it was only by luck that no one was killed. Of course some Jews have been avoiding military service but that is true of all sorts, and I am not the only Jew here from Leeds by any means. One chap I met had his shop wrecked. His wife and children were in a room directly above when it happened, so you can imagine what he felt when he heard. One of his wife's brothers was killed out here a few months ago as well. Apparently the Leylands looked like a battlefield after the second night.

I am doing alright here. We are back from the line and having quite a nice time of it, helped by your parcel. The weather is fine and there is time to sit around with one's pals, though of course we know that we will be going back up again some time. I met a Jewish chaplain the other day. He was going down the lines looking for Jews. He was rather a good fellow, I thought. He said last year he held some well-attended New Year and Yom Kippur services in this sector. Three hundred men came for Yom Kippur, it would have been more but quite a few went over the top that morning. The services were held in a cinema which everyone of course immediately called the cinemagogue. He has conducted quite a lot of Jewish burials, he said. Hopefully, I will be able to go to his services when that time of year comes again.

I heard a funny story the other day. A Jewish fellow I met told me how when they had been moving through German trenches on an attack his pals had made him go first, shouting to the Germans to come out in Yiddish and they had understood and did as they were told.

Well, I had better stop, I've got kit inspection soon and have to clean my rifle.

I send my fond regards to you all and thank you again for the parcel.

Yours sincerely,
Sam

Sheina

Riga, 1918

Mameh, a letter has come, a letter from Israel. From your son Israel, Mameh, in South Africa. No, Mameh, he's not a rabbi. He's written a letter, he wants to know if we're still alive. I know, Mameh, there have been problems with letters. The Russians wouldn't allow any letters in Yiddish, they said the Jews were spying, that we were sending messages to the Germans. And now the Germans are fighting the British so no letters can come from South Africa. This one has come through Holland. Israel must know someone in Holland he sent it through. Now, you want to ask questions, Mameh, or you want me to tell you what's in this letter from Israel? From Israel, Mameh. How can Israel save us from the Russians? We're not under the Russians any more. The Germans came. Don't you remember, Mameh? We hid in the cellar for three days with poor Chaya's pains coming on. Only by the grace of God was little Esther not born in that cellar. Esther, Mameh, my daughter Chaya's baby Esther, you were holding her only an hour ago. You don't remember how she was almost born in that cellar while the shooting and bombing was going on? You don't remember what it was like when we came out? If God could give me such a memory that I could forget what I saw, people lying dead in the street, holes where houses had been. God smiled on us that a bomb did not fall on our building and kill us all. Nobody wants to kill us any more, Mameh. God be thanked the war is finished for us now. You don't remember how the Russians ran away and the Germans came in smiling and waving and saying Gut morgen to everybody? Some of their officers even are Jewish. Life is better now, we can breathe without fear, Lipmann can do a little business, there's no profit in it but at least he can keep the factory alive until the war is finished. Now enough, Mameh, you want to hear what the letter says? Eli is doing well at school. Rosa has won a place at university. You hear that Mameh? She is one of the first girls in Pretoria to win a place at the university. Meyer has two children now. Isn't that good news Mameh? You have another granddaughter we didn't even know about. Boris is still childless it seems. Boris, Mameh. Don't speak like that about your son, Mameh. Now what else? The rest is mostly about this Britisher Balfour who wrote this letter promising Britain would help the Jews get back the Land of Israel. No, Mameh, the Messiah has not come, you have not missed the Messiah. Yes, Mameh, I will tell you when the Messiah comes. Israel isn't waiting for the Messiah, Mameh, he wants to rebuild the Land of Israel without the Messiah. He writes they had a procession through the streets of Pretoria to celebrate this letter from the Britisher Balfour with flags and music. Pretoria, Mameh, that's where Israel lives. No, Mameh, Israel is not a rabbi. He works with Boris and Meyer in the meat business. Yes, Mameh, it is good Israel is working with his brothers. Yes, Mameh, with his brains and education he will be sure to make the business a big success. Yes, Mameh, I know, you have told me many times, the Rabbis kissed him at his barmitzvah. Yes, Mameh, I remember, you always said he would be a distinguished Jew among Jews.

Zion

From The Zionist Record, 1920–5

PICNIC BESIDE THE LAKE

The Pretoria Zionist Guild is holding its First Annual Picnic on Sunday, 22 November. Among the entertainments will be boating, swimming, music and games for the children. Gentlemen, 10/6; Ladies, 7/6; Children, 5s. Tickets from Mr. I. Dunsky, Secretary.

CONTRIBUTIONS TO THE SHEKEL FUND

Pretoria – H. Gorfunkel, 5s.; G. Sherman, 2s. 6d.; T. Lazarus, 6d.; L. Drobis, 5s.; I. Dunsky, 7s. 6d.; Mrs M. Klassman, £1.; F. Manaswitz, 7s. 4d.; J. Shoob, 3s.; Z. Matz, 9d.

ALL-NIGHT VIGIL

Two officers of the Pretoria Zionist Guild have shown their fealty to the national cause in a most commendable way.

After the Guild's annual bazaar concern was voiced, in the light of recent burglaries in the city, about the security of the takings until they could be deposited at the bank in the morning. In consequence, the Treasurer, Mr. L. Drobis, and the Secretary, Mr. I. Dunsky, sat up through the night to guard the money, keeping themselves awake by drinking coffee, playing chess, and discussing various topics of Zionist interest. The handsome sum of £57. 8s. 2d. is now safely swelling the coffers of the National Fund.

SOME ASPECTS OF ZIONISM

The Pretoria Jewish Literary Club met to hear a lecture by Mr. S. Blau on 'Some Aspects of Zionism'. Unfortunately the inclement weather caused the audience to be smaller than might have been wished, for the paper was a most instructive and illuminating one. Thanks were proposed by Mr. I. Dunsky, the chairman, to Mr. Blau for his trouble in coming specially from Johannesburg, and to Mrs P. Dunsky for providing the much-enjoyed refreshments.

A BAKER'S SCORE

'The Zionist Record' would like to thank all readers who took part in the highly successful drive to enlist new subscribers. A total of 324 new subscriptions have now been paid up. The winners of the competition to bring in the most subscriptions are: first prize, a priceless Maccabean coin, Mr.

D. Torph, with 22 new subscribers, 21 of them customers at his Johannesburg bakery; second prize, 'Graetz's History of the Jews' (6 vols), Mrs Debbie Greenberg, a secretary, also from Johannesburg, with 11 new subscriptions; and third prize, 'Jewish Contributions to Civilization: an Estimate,' by Joseph Jacobs, D. Litt., Mr. I. Dunsky, Secretary of the Pretoria Zionist Guild, with a total of 7 new subscriptions.

PRETORIA NOTES

The annual meeting of the Pretoria Zionist Guild was held, at which the resignation of the President, Mr. P. Meskin, due to ill health, was sadly accepted. As a token of great appreciation for his ardent and zealous work for the cause, the retiring President was unanimously elected honorary member of the committee for life. A keen interest was also taken in the election of office bearers for the year ahead. These are as follows: Mr. L. Drobis, President; Mr. I. Dunsky, Treasurer; Mr. G. Sherman, Secretary. Members of the committee are: Mr. T. Lazarus, Mr. S. Zolty, Mr. W. Siegenberg, Mr. J. Shoob, Mr. P. Meskin (honorary, life). The meeting concluded with a final vote of thanks to the outgoing President, and terminated with the singing of the 'Hatikvah'.

RECORD HELPS RECOVER MONEY, BENEFITS JNF

The Jewish homeland has benefited from a happy occurrence following a mention of Mr. I. Dunsky of the Pretoria

Zionist Guild in the 'Record'. Some years ago Mr. Dunsky was generous enough to guarantee a loan of £5 from the Gemilut Hasidim in Germiston, where he was then residing, to a peddler who subsequently defaulted on the sum. After Mr. Dunsky's mention in the 'Record' the aforesaid peddler, now clearly a man of greater substance than before, wrote to Mr. Dunsky enclosing a cheque to repay the loan, which Mr. Dunsky has most kindly signed over to the National Fund.

PRETORIA YOUNG ZIONISTS IN CONCERT

A concert of music and orations by the Pretoria Ozrei Zion, whose members are drawn from the young Jewish people of the city, raised £37. 2s. for the national cause. The Flatnower sisters, Madeline and Molly, opened the concert with a piano duet that was a rare treat. Following was Miss R. Shoob who rendered several modern airs, including 'A lovely place to be,' in her best style. Master S. Siegenberg made a recital in Hebrew which met with a cordial reception, while Master N. Drobis told a lengthy tale about the Maccabeans, and appealed to his fellow young Zionists to be brave and good Jews. The concert was concluded with a series of Oriental songs by Miss Annie Gurland, accompanied efficiently on the piano by Miss Rosa Dunsky. Special thanks are due to all who helped to make the function such a success.

MISAPPREHENSION THAT SHOULD BE STAMPED OUT

Mr. I. Dunsky, Treasurer of the Pretoria Zionist Guild, has drawn our attention to a matter that could lead to anti-Jewish feelings. A complaint was recently made to Mr. Dunsky by a Gentile who bought a Jewish National Fund stamp under the misapprehension that it was an ordinary postage stamp and was distressed when the letter on which he had placed it was returned. Mr. Dunsky suggests that while Jewish store-owners should be commended for displaying the National Fund stamps in prominent positions, care should be taken to inform customers that the stamps are purely for ornamental purposes and have no currency with the Post Office.

A NOVEL IDEA

The ballroom of the Pretoria Hotel paid witness to one of the most novel events of recent years, in the shape of the Pretoria Zionist Guild's book dance, an idea which might happily be replicated by other guilds and societies. The guests came dressed as the titles of books, and the dance proved both most enjoyable and highly educational as to the great wealth of literature we have in the world, as well as raising good money for the Jewish homeland. Refreshments were freely distributed through the evening and there was dancing to the strains of Blum's Band until two o'clock in the morning. At midnight, the winners were judged and prizes awarded to:

1. 'Mating Song', Master R. L. Millett; 2. 'The Breakfast of Birds', Miss R. Dunsky; 3. 'Jocund Day', Master R. Fiewel.

THE LATE MR. L. DROBIS

At an extraordinary meeting of the Pretoria Zionist Guild the sudden and untimely death of Mr. L. Drobis, President, was lamented. Many warm and laudatory words were spoken about the deceased gentleman, who had been a leading member of the Jewish community in Pretoria and one of the most respected communal workers in the Transvaal since his arrival in the capital eighteen years ago. Condolences were made to Mr. Drobis's widow, Mrs Rachel Drobis, and his three children, viz; Mrs Milly Zolty and Herman and Nathaniel Drobis. In a sombre vote, the following officers were elected: Mr. I. Dunsky, President; Mr. G. Sherman, Treasurer; Mr. J. Shoob, Secretary.

FIRST WOMEN BACHELORS

Two members of the Pretoria Ozrei Zion have become the first women to be awarded Bachelor of Arts degrees from Pretoria University. Miss Annie Gurland and Miss Rosa Dunsky, the latter the daughter of Mr. I. Dunsky, President of the Pretoria Zionist Guild, both graduated with degrees in English and History. Miss Dunsky applied to join the Civil Service and upon graduating has been accepted into the Office of the Government Buyer.

EINSTEIN THE JEW

Readers in the Pretoria region may have noticed a recent exchange of letters and articles in the 'Pretoria Argus' over the nationality of Mr. Albert Einstein. For those in other regions, the debate was initiated by a letter to the 'Argus' from Mr. I. Dunsky, President of the Pretoria Zionist Guild, pointing out that when covering Mr. Einstein's journey to America the newspaper had described him as a Swiss national but failed to mention that he is a Jew. We do not see it our place to get involved in this argument, or even to comment on the rights or wrongs of instigating such a debate, but we would like to bring to notice the fact that if there was a Jewish state Mr. Einstein could be a national of, such debate would be unnecessary.

LEVIN IN PRETORIA

Thursday 12 March will go down as a red letter day in the annals of Pretoria Jewry, for that was the day Mr. Shmarya Levin spoke in the capital. The first senior emissary from the Zionist Organization in Europe to visit Pretoria brought out the largest gathering of Zionists ever seen in the city, and the crowds were not disappointed. From the moment Mr. Levin began talking the audience was spellbound and his conclusion was greeted with such a roar of appreciation and clapping that older members had to cover their ears for fear of damage to their ear drums. With the greatest wit and oratorial skills Mr. Levin updated the audience as to the state of Zionism and appealed to the Jews of South Africa to support the Keren Hayesod, the newly established fund for the development of a Jewish national home in Palestine. It was an appeal that could not be, and was not, ignored, to the tune of pledges of more than £150 that evening alone. Mr. I. Dunsky, President of the Pretoria Zionist Guild, proposed a hearty vote of thanks both to Mr. Levin and to the Zionists of Pretoria for responding so enthusiastically to Mr. Levin's call, and offered up to auction a Gloria Lamp which had been donated for this purpose, and which raised a further £17. 85d.

JEWISH HOMELAND BENEFITS TWICE

The magnificence of South African Jewry's response to the target of £250,000 set by the Zionist Organization in Europe as this country's contribution to the Keren Hayesod has yielded a bonus for the Jewish homeland in the form of a 'donation' from an unlikely source. In the course of a family debate, Mr. M. Dunsky of Johannesburg, a sceptic when it comes to Zionism, expressed doubt that South African Jewry would contribute £50,000 let alone £250,000 to the Keren Hayesod. His brother, Mr. I. Dunsky, President of the Zionist Guild, offered the opposite opinion and the two agreed upon a wager, which, with the fund recently passing £50,000, was won by Mr. I. Dunsky, who has most generously signed over to the Fund his winnings, viz; the sum of £5.

PRETORIA JEW TO STUDY IN ENGLAND

Mr. Eli Dunsky, son of Mr. I. Dunsky, President of the Pretoria Zionist Guild, is to travel to England to continue his studies in the field of chemistry at Imperial College in London. Mr. Dunsky graduated with a Bachelor of Science degree in chemistry from Pretoria University, with distinction in organic chemistry, and we wish him all good luck in his ventures overseas.

ZIONISTS REPRESENTED AT GLITTERING EVENT

Mr. I. Dunsky, President of the Pretoria Zionist Guild, and Mrs Dunsky, along with The Rev. L. Matz of the Pretoria Congregation and Mrs Matz, were among the guests last week at the State Ball held in the capital in honour of H.R.H. the Prince of Wales. The glittering occasion, which was the culmination of His Royal Highness's month-long tour of South Africa, was unquestionably the premier social event ever held in this country. Hosted by His Excellency the Governor General, the Earl of Athlone and H.R.H. Princess Alice, Countess of Athlone, guests were drawn from the senior echelons of the diplomatic, administrative, political, military, business and religious communities, as well as high society. Mr. Dunsky, reporting to 'The Zionist

Record', confirmed newspaper accounts that Government House was decorated throughout with dazzling lights and beautiful native flowers, and that the drinks and buffet supper were of the highest order. Mr. Dunsky could not however comment on the dancing which was reported to have continued until 2.30 a.m., as he and Mrs Dunsky left some time before midnight.

2 Judges

From Pretoria News, *1927*

Israel Dunsky, former manager of the Pretoria branch of Dunsky Brothers Meats and Hides Consolidated, was yesterday fined £10 or twenty-eight days hard labour for selling diseased meat to the Prisons Department. The prosecution was conducted by Inspector Dobson and evidence was given by Inspector Bemister that the meat had been illegally tampered with in the shape of washing, rubbing or stripping to disguise the evidence of its diseased condition.

A previous conviction of the defendant for Sunday trading in Germiston was recorded.

Boris

Johannesburg, 1927

Some days I wish I had never sold my horse. I could saddle
up and ride out onto the veldt again. Take a blanket with
me, sleep out under the stars, forget all these troubles. It's
never been the same buying livestock at the market. You
make your bid, sign your name, that's the last you see of the
animals. When I was buying from farms I would ride for
days over the veldt building up a herd, then drive it slowly
back so as not to lose the flesh I had paid for. When I was
hungry I killed a sheep and made a fire to cook it on. The
flames die down you dig a hole and put in the sheep's head
and fill it with hot ashes, the next morning you dig it up
again and the skin falls off and the flesh around the skull,
you have never tasted anything like it, so sweet and soft.

There was a Jew had a little farm right out in the back
country. Twenty years or more he'd been there, he hardly

remembered he was a Jew and everyone else had forgotten if they ever knew. They called him by some Boer name, he lived like a Boer, spoke their language, he'd even married a Boer girl in one of their churches and had little Boer children. Whether they knew or not, they treated him like one of their own. They always liked us those country Boers, called us the People of the Book. On one farm I bought from there was a girl I used to talk to sometimes, before I met Malka. A big, healthy, quiet girl. One day she took me around the back of the farmhouse, there was a sloot ran there, it had been raining and raining and the sloot had turned into a torrent and she wanted to show me something, so I stood there with her until we saw it, a black snake washing past, swirling in the water, then another, and another, and another.

They liked it the Boers when I told them a little of the Bible in Hebrew, tears would come into their eyes and they would beg me to say more. I would tell them to wait until I brought my brother with me, he could recite the whole book for them, but Israel would never leave the shop.

Why some people have to be so stubborn I don't know. It's like I tell Malka, if there's something you can do to help yourself do it, if not don't let it eat you up. I took her to see the best doctors in Johannesburg and they all said the same thing. Something twisted inside her you can't untwist. What good does it do to keep worrying over it until it gives her another headache and she has to go upstairs and lie down with a cloth soaked in vinegar on her brow?

I'm not one to bend with every storm that sweeps across the veldt, but when it blows strong you find some shelter and wait for it to pass over, then you can continue on your way. But not Israel. Israel has to stand up in the dust and make a point of principle to the wind. It lost him the first job he had in South Africa. I didn't like the trick that old man who owned the old clothes store played on the Kaffirs either, putting a wallet with some washers into the pocket of a coat so they would think they were getting a secret bargain. But it was enough to give them back their money and take back the coat. Israel didn't have to lecture the old man.

It's like I told him a hundred times. Don't argue with Max. You argue with Max, he only shouts louder and starts hopping up and down until his trousers are climbing up his legs. Let him shout until he's used up all his breath, then you carry on with whatever it was you were doing in the first place. Max likes to hear his own voice, he doesn't mean half of what he says. Like at my house when he asked Rosa if she would put in a word for him at the Government Buyer's Office. Israel stands up, picks up his coat, tells his family they're leaving, he's not eating lunch with someone who wants to corrupt his daughter. I had to follow him outside and stand in the rain begging him to come back. Don't go, I told him, you will give Malka another headache, at least you have got children to argue about. There was nothing in it anyway. Max doesn't need Rosa to put in a good word with the Buyer's Office, he's got his own people there.

It was the same with the Kaffir who cut off his finger. I'm not saying Israel wasn't right, you can't get rid of a man while he's still bleeding, even if it is all over your meat. But if Max gets it into his head that he's going to fire someone he's going to fire him. You don't argue with him, you let him fire the Kaffir, you slip him a few shillings for the doctor, send him home for a few weeks and tell him to come back when it is healed. The fuss Israel made that Kaffir could never come back, I had to find him a job at the market in Johannesburg.

The way I see it, you've got to know how to look at a problem. It's like livestock. Some animals look big on the outside but when you cut them open they're all fat and bones underneath, their bellies swollen with gas and water. I can look at a cow and in one minute tell you to five pounds how much meat it's got on it.

If Israel had left well alone nothing would have happened. The meat wasn't going to poison the Kaffirs, they eat meat ten times more rotten than that every day in their villages. But when he found out Max had gone behind his back and sent it to the prison, he had to go down there and tell them. So whose fault was it Israel is up in front of the magistrate? No. Not Israel. Zionism is up in front of the magistrate. It's not him on trial, it's Zionism. It gets written in the newspaper, it looks bad on Zionism. He's got a position in the community. He didn't get invited with the Prince of Wales because he's manager of Dunsky Brothers. If people think the President of the Zionists in the capital is crooked, they stop giving money. Max said it's a bonus then, not only does Dunsky Brothers make money but South Africa's Jews save some too.

As stubborn as fat-tailed sheep, the pair of them. Whether Israel resigned or Max fired him I don't know. Max won't talk about it and Israel won't talk to me at all. I telephone him he puts down the handset, I go to his door I can hear him saying he doesn't have any brothers. I am not walking into a house where I'm not welcome. I've got my own problems. It's only from Malka speaking to Pearl on the telephone I even heard the happy news.

Rosa

Pretoria

My Dearest Eli,

Please do not be too angry and upset with Dadda and Mamma. You know what they are like with any change to our lives, however good. Give them time and I am sure they will be looking forward to meeting Golda and welcoming her into the family, as I am so very much myself. Of course behind their reaction is their fear that now they will see you only once or twice more in their lives, which I must admit I share myself, but that is no reason for you not to follow your own road. As for your giving up your studies, I told them that is your choice to make as well, and it is not as if you are asking them to support you but are looking for a job and have probably found a very good one by now.

I hope you will forgive me for going on about this when all I am yearning to do is share with you in your happiness, but I want to make sure we do not have any more splits in this family. I am not sure you have properly realized how things have been here. With your studies I didn't want to burden you and Dadda would never admit that he is in trouble, but I think you should know what difficult times we have been through, even if they are somewhat improved now. In the weeks after Dadda's resignation I was really quite worried about him. I would come home from work and find him walking up and down the verandah deep in thought or talking to himself. His stomach was acting up again and he put himself on a diet of only milk, you can imagine how much that distressed Mamma. As for Mamma, however much she has always complained about Aunt Malka their friendship has been very important to her, and now that is limited to furtive conversations on the telephone. Dadda will still not allow our uncles' names even to be mentioned in the house and Mamma refers to them only as the 'ignorant swine'.

I think it is to Dadda's enormous credit the way he has responded. Reading between the lines of what Mamma reports from Malka it seems Uncle Max got quite a shock when Dadda started up in opposition to Dunsky Brothers and particularly when he heard that Dadda had leased a Ford lorry to deliver his meat, while Dunsky Brothers is still using horses and carts. But Dadda has had to work very hard for a man of his age and his principles have not exactly helped him. When they heard about his new business half the employees of Dunsky Brothers, black and white, came to him offering their services but he would not take on a single one of them. He told them he could not offer them the safe jobs they had at Dunsky Brothers and sent them all back, though how safe they actually are there can be gauged from how many good ex-Dunsky Brothers workers he has been able to employ. Without them I don't think he could have got off the ground, so that is something good that has come out of Uncle Max's policy of firing someone every week! Then of course he refused to solicit business from his old customers, which wouldn't have left him with much of a market if some of them, particularly the Jewish ones, hadn't insisted on going with him to Pretoria Meats & Hides. The business does just about seem to be paying its way. Dadda was lucky to find such a good buyer in the old Gentile, who is apparently every bit as good as Uncle Boris. But as I said he is having to work very hard and with his premises so close to Dunsky Brothers he keeps catching glimpses of our uncles which cannot help his equilibrium. And all this on top of terrible money pressure, as he has had to mortgage both his plot of land at Lion's Bridge and the house, which worries Mamma greatly. Everything now depends on this business, if it fails God knows what will happen, if it succeeds then perhaps he and Mamma really will be able to retire to the Land of Israel.

Dear brother, I hope you do not think worse of me for this letter. My only aim is to make it easier for you to think more favourably of our parents. Could you bring yourself to write to them in conciliatory fashion? That must be your priority, though of course when you have time I would love my own letter. I am dying to hear more about Golda and her family and your plans. I send you all the happiness in the world.

With my love to you and Golda,

Rosa

8 January 1928

My Dear Brother,

How strange it is to be sitting writing this letter to you at the very moment you are being married. I cannot pretend that it is not heartbreaking to be so far away from you on your special day, but I am full of gladness for both of you. You cannot imagine how happy I was when your letter arrived with the snaps of you and Golda. I can tell you that you did yourself a great service. Mamma spent an hour on the telephone with Aunt Malka and Dadda sat and studied the snap for a whole minute. How charming Golda looks. Her face is so friendly and homely that when I meet her I am certain I shall feel I have known her all my life. From your description she sounds such a very special little person, and her sister Zelda too. How nice it must be to have a sister you are so close to.

Of course as you can imagine for Dadda the most important thing is your job. I do not see why you have to apologize about it being a varnish factory, as varnish is a very useful and necessary product and your talents will be well used in its production. Dadda certainly thinks it sounds a good business with prospects, and would talk of nothing else all evening. I can admit now that I was secretly worried that you would out of necessity go to work for Golda's sister's husband. I am sure he is a very good employer and he certainly sounds very successful, but I couldn't bear the thought of you becoming dependent on relations. I do not have to tell you that I am sure you will do brilliantly. I have looked up Gravesend in the atlas. Despite its name it looks as though it must be a beautiful place.

This is not going to be a long letter. I do not want to bore you with one of my 'novels' and I have promised to take Mamma to the Bio tonight, though there is something I am planning to tell you about myself at some point. All that is left is to wish you and Golda a long and happy life together, in which you will always consider each other not only as man and wife but as dear and true friends and helpmeets. As soon as you can please write about the wedding and your honeymoon and life in Gravesend, and of course send any photographs you can. We shall be waiting with baited breath.

I send you and Golda all my love,

Rosa

30 April 1928

My dearest Eli,

Do you remember I wrote not long ago that there was something I would tell you. Well, I am going to write about it now. In fact I was about to do so but then you wrote with your news of Golda and I did not want to steal your thunder with my own story of love and marriage. That is right, Eli, I have a boy of my own and I am planning my own wedding.

I have known him for some time and our decision to get married is not new, but first there was the trouble with Dunsky Brothers, and then Mamma's and Dadda's reaction to your plans, and I didn't dare stir things up any further, but now that they seem to have accepted your situation I cannot wait any longer myself. I am writing to let you know about Lazar, but also to tell someone before I go into the lion's den, as I am going to bring him to dinner on Sunday.

Fortunately at least Dadda will not be able to say we are not in a position to get married, for Lazar has a lucrative profession of sorts – he is a very fine photographer.

He comes from a good family in a village that is only a couple of hundred miles from Dadda's. It was only because the village was burnt down during the war and they had to flee that he gave up his schooling and determined to learn some trade or profession and so keep his elderly parents going. He was sixteen years old when this happened and came to South Africa a few years after the war. He is very far indeed from being an ignoramus and is also very artistic. As a matter of fact he has modelled a few figures and had determined to devote his life to art when he met me.

That knocked all his previous plans on the head and he decided that as he wished to marry me he must be in a position to keep me, and though the sum of money he had was negligible he borrowed some more and opened up a studio in Joh'burg, and has been making remarkable progress. He is not only making a living but is doing well – very well, as a matter of fact. He borrowed about £200, every penny of which he has now paid off, and last month he made £80 sheer profit, so you see there would be no material drawbacks to our getting married. He has prepared a set of accounts which we are going to take to show Dadda.

So you see I am well armed against any objection that Mamma and Dadda may make, though that does not mean I am expecting the best. Wish me luck.

I hope that things are going well with you. I constantly gaze at your snaps and long to see and embrace the originals. I feel that now, especially, Golda would be such a comfort.

I cannot write any more, I am too nervous.

Your loving sister,

Rosa

12 May 1928

Dearly Beloved Brother,

So, now we have both upset the apple cart, though what Mamma and Dadda can have expected I don't know. That we would marry a boy and girl of their picking? If so, why did they not invite the marriage broker to come and drink tea and show them credentials? Presumably he would not have been able to find a husband for the monster in human shape it seems I am for wanting to have a happy life with a man I love.

Oh, brother, I pray to God that as long as I live I shall never have to endure a day like Sunday again. Lazar is a little on the short side and slightly built and you know Mamma's passion for solid, well-fed looking people. (He does every scrap of his work himself and never leaves the studio during the day and I am sure often forgets meal times.) He has an olive complexion and his hair on top is very thin. It used to be very greasy, so he would wash it with washing soda and this is the result. He hadn't slept a wink the previous night. Suffice it to say that he did not look his best.

Poor boy. As soon as Mamma saw him, I knew that things were not going well. She kept making faces and pretending not to hear what he said or to misunderstand him. She piled his plate ridiculously high and when he left some small piece of gristle on the edge of the plate she looked at it with a mixture of satisfaction and triumph. After dinner we fled into the drawing-room while Dadda went for his lie down and waited and waited. In the end I realized they were not going to come to us and we went out onto the verandah where Mamma was. She began to speak to Lazar, complaining indirectly of me, of you, of our lack of gratitude and consideration for our parents. Poor Mamma, she absolutely cannot see anyone's point of view except her own. However he answered her at first in English, and then in Yiddish, and he speaks it in a very charming fashion and Mamma despite herself began to respond to him.

Afterwards Dadda came out and Lazar spoke and spoke to them, and showed Dadda his accounts, and a medical letter attesting that he is in good health that he had insisted on getting for the occasion, until at last Dadda said he had no objections. I so wanted to leave with Lazar and comfort him, but I felt I had to stay. As soon as he left Mamma started talking about how she had always hoped I would marry a doctor or a lawyer, which I told her was too much seeing as how she always goes on about the millionaires she turned down in Leeds for love of Dadda. Of course Mamma said that was different though how it was different I do not know. Luckily, Dadda stepped in and said that as far as he was concerned Lazar was a 'ganz feine mensch.'

So, Eli, the deed is done. You do not know how lucky you were not to be at home when you married. At least now I have their agreement, if not exactly their approval, and we can carry on with making our arrangements.

Your loving sister,

Rosa

30 August 1928

My Dear Eli,

Thank you very much for your letter, though I must tell you now that it looks like the wedding will have to be delayed. Dadda's business is in serious trouble. I cannot remember now if anyone wrote to you about Dadda's buyer, the elderly Gentile, dying suddenly. I am afraid to say that I was too caught up with my own concerns to fully appreciate its significance, which is all too clear now. It happened two months ago and has been causing Dadda all sorts of problems. Good buyers are very rare and afterwards Dadda tried using another buyer, but he has his own business and only gave Dadda the leftovers, so Dadda dropped him and has since been doing the buying himself. He is not an expert and it means he is having to do everything and has been working all hours of the day. Uncle Boris sent a message through Malka that he would be willing to do Dadda's buying on the quiet if necessary, but Dadda would not hear of it. The result is that Pretoria Meats & Hides is struggling and Dadda is exhausted and very troubled. I have considered giving up my job to help him, but the truth is the family finances are so stretched that we need my income. I have even been borrowing little bits of money from Lazar and slipping them into the household kitty so that Mamma does not run short. Under the circumstances we really do not feel we should go ahead with the wedding, even though Lazar could afford to pay for it all himself. It is really quite desperate at home and there being so little that Mamma and I can do. If Dadda were at least to give up his Zionist activities temporarily it might give him some breathing space, but he will not consider it. I think they are even more important to him at this moment.

For God's sake do not write about this, even in a letter to me, but I am considering biting the bullet and going to talk secretly to the 'ignorant swine.' Uncle Max has done this family great harm and I am not sure I can ever forgive him, but he is not such a bad man and I am going to appeal to his better nature. Or if that does not work use my wiles. The other night I woke thinking there was a burglar in the house, it was Dadda, sitting on the verandah reading the Bible in his sing-song voice. He has been reading over and over again his favourite bits, the Psalms, and especially Isaiah and anything else about returning to the Land of Israel.

I know it is selfish but I must have one little lament to my brother about my wedding, as I have been waiting so long. Lazar and I have found a very nice place to live in Johannesburg. It is a flatlet in a newly built block, it is still being finished actually, and we will be the very first people to rent it. It is called a bachelor flat, though actually these flats are rented more by young couples and elderly people. There is a bath and a little hall and it will be furnished by the time we move in. The kitchen even has an electric cooker, where I will be able to essay a little cooking and find out whether I am as hopeless as I think I am. Perhaps it would be a blessing after all for Lazar if the wedding is delayed!

Well, that is our situation. I hope that everything is going better for you than for us and that I have not bored you too much with all our troubles. I send you both my love.

Your Rosa

17 November 1928

My Dear Brother,

Please don't be worried by what I am going to say as the doctor has assured us it is not serious, but Dadda has had a collapse. It happened three days ago and I am glad I did not send a telegram to you as he is much better now and is sitting up in bed at home and getting up himself to go to the lavatory. According to the doctor it is quite common in people who have been working and worrying too hard and then stop for some reason. The body keeps going and going until it can relax and then it gives out temporarily. You see Dadda's business is sold. Uncle Max and Uncle Boris have bought it and the collapse happened the day after the contracts were signed. So really this letter should not worry you but reassure you that things are better here.

Please let me swear you again to secrecy, for Dadda has no idea of the part I played in the affair. He thinks the offer came unsolicited from Uncle Max and I think would not have accepted it if he had known I had prompted it. I told you I was thinking about going to see Uncle Max. After much thought I went first to Uncle Boris to get him on my side. That was not difficult at all, he was greatly relieved by my visit and in fact tears came to his eyes when I told him why I had come. I felt loving towards the old ox. More like an old bear.

Uncle Max was not so easy. He was very gracious to me when I first arrived, but then became his worst self when he found out why I had come, but I would not take no for an answer. I think you would have been proud to see me, Eli. I charmed him and praised him and played on his guilt in equal measure and in the end he agreed to my plan. As I said, they have given Dadda a good price for the business, more than it is really worth as it was in a state of collapse, but of course much less than he really deserves for all the years he put into Dunsky Brothers. Nevertheless Dadda was satisfied and I think enormously relieved, which ironically led to his collapse.

What this all means for the wedding I have not even thought about. Of course the priority is Dadda's health and, if necessary, we will postpone it again. Luckily the invitations have not yet gone out and Lazar will do whatever I want. He only wants what is best for me and therefore will accept whatever is best for Dadda.

Well, that is all Eli. I wanted you to know what has been happening here. Please be reassured that all seems well now and perhaps we are moving into better times.

Your loving sister,

Rosa

16 January 1929

My Dearest Eli and Golda,

So here we are on our honeymoon! We didn't delay the wedding and it turned out to be the right decision. The coast here is the most beautiful place on God's earth and the hotel is like paradise, even if we have Mamma and Dadda with us. Yes, you can believe your eyes. I didn't have the time to write to you about it, it all happened at the last minute, but before I explain, let me tell you about the wedding itself.

I believe it turned out to be quite a success. It was a luncheon affair at the Jewish Communal Centre, all catered, which was very nice, though Mamma insisted on adding her own specialities to the menu. I had been simply dreading it but in the end I actually enjoyed myself. The bonus of the deal with Dadda's business was that our uncles and their families all came and in retrospect I don't think it would have been the same without them. They were very generous with their gifts, Dunsky Brothers supplied the meat for free, and for all Uncle Max, in particular, has done I was glad that they were there. I think Dadda was too, otherwise he would have brooded about them. The only sadness was your and Golda's absence, but we cannot have everything.

Mamma after all the fuss she made could not have behaved more perfectly. She looked beautiful and completely outshone her daughter. Lazar's relations were especially taken with her and she was almost charming to them. Dadda moved through the gathering with his blue box. I believe he collected about twenty pounds, which seemed to please him even more than the fact of his daughter's marriage!

Now let me explain about Mamma and Dadda. It was Lazar actually who invited them to come with us, he is such a sweet man. The doctor on one of his visits suggested that Dadda should have a holiday and when I reported this to Lazar, he said immediately that they should accompany us.

At first Dadda would not hear of it, but the doctor was quite insistent, and Mamma put her foot down too, and with the business sold Dadda for once could not use work as an excuse. It is really not so bad having them here. They have been very good at looking after themselves and giving Lazar and me time to spend alone together. Mamma is quite content to be in the lap of luxury and has loved going in the sea, even if not in her nightdress! Even Dadda has begun to grow accustomed to being on the first holiday of his life.

The first day he spent sitting on the verandah with his nose in a book, ignoring the view completely and when we finally managed to get him down to the beach on the second day, he sat on the stones in his coat and hat and carried on reading his book there. It is very hot and everyone bathes, and they looked at him quite strangely.

The day before yesterday, though, he suddenly announced he was going for a swim. Mamma had bought him a bathing suit before they left and to me it was more extraordinary to see him dressed in that than sitting among the bathers in his coat and hat. You should have seen him getting into the water, Eli, it was very comic but also quite touching. First he stood in the shallows and splashed water over each part of his body in turn as if he were washing himself. Apparently this is to prevent the cold water being too much of a shock. Then he slowly dipped himself in. You know how he has always said what a strong swimmer he was, well he does swim well, but in quite a strange fashion, on his side waving the upper arm like a windmill. He swam for ten minutes up and down alongside the beach, and did the same yesterday. It was quite something to see.

Being Dadda of course he finds it hard to relax. He keeps quizzing Lazar about our flat. He was quite taken with the building when he came to see it and keeps asking Lazar how many flats there are, how many shops, what the rent is, the footage and everything. While everyone else sits around reading their newspapers and novels he is busy scratching a pencil on paper making calculations about his land at Lion's Bridge. Whether anything will come of it, at least it allows him to claim he is not wasting his time completely.

So you see how it is Eli, even when I write a letter from my honeymoon most of it is about Dadda. I can assure you that Lazar and I are enjoying ourselves, going for walks along the beautiful coast, bathing and simply being happy together. We have another five days here and then we are heading straight to Joh'burg. It all seems so unreal. Can I really be married and all my troubles be over?

I send you both heaps and heaps of love and good wishes, as does Lazar.

Your Rosa

Song of Songs

Pretoria

21/8/29

Dear Son,

your letter I have received and read it with great pleasure. I & Mother are very hapy with your news. You must give our congratulations to your Wife. We hope before long to make aquaintence with her. I am satsfied you are working hard. The world at this present time is not in love with work therefor those who work are sure to suceed. Do what work you have to do and do it well. Abought myself thank you for your inquire. I am quite well ocupied. The plans for building up my land at Lions Bridge are going ahead. The specfications have been aproved by the planing board and I am pleased the Bank has given me the loan I Need. The Manager said he would not have alowed such a sum to any one but he made an exeption of my name and reputation.

Whatever some people might say Honesty and Principle in business can yeald benefits. The Architect is inteligent with modern ideas. The Plan is for a 3 story building 6 shops ground floor and 12 flats 2 floors. In each flat electric stove and electric refrigerator. It will cost more but the rental will be hire. These blocks are going up in Joburg but none in Pretoria so I think it will lett readily. Of course there will not be much money for us in the first few years but in time I hope there will be enough for my Cherished Hope of setlement in Ertz Israel. I am indulging in Dreams. But I hope it will become True this time. When I bought the land at Lions Bridge it was a wasteland with rats rocks and only the shoemakers store. Pearl said it was foolish when we didnt have the money to build on it I told her it was an investment I am proved wright. The shoemaker will not lose out either. Next week I hope the work will go out to tenter. You wright in your letter abought your name hindering you in getting another job well you must make your own mind up. It shows you our position either we must sufer for admiting openly what we are or adopt subtrefuges which criple us Moraly and turn us into Deceivers the answer to all that is Ertz Israel. I hope you read the economic crisis is over there. Now the Jewish Agency is sett up American Notables are on board and funds will flow the future is bright. New industries are spring up and thousands dunams of land are planted with orange orchards. I am happy I have contributed a few of these dunams with my eforts. Last month was the twentieth aniversary of Tel-Aviv. It was sand now it has 40,000 people almost 100% Jews, the police, the courts, the newspapers, theatre, opera all are by Jews for Jews. In the SA Jewish Chronicle I read there are cement, soap and chemical manure factories in Tel-Aviv so there would be openings for a chemist as good as varnish, especialy now you are starting a family. The troubles with Arabs are past it is peaceful there and safe. Weizmann wants 20,000 cha-lutzim a year that is the life-blood of Zionism. That is for you to think abought. You would not have to worry abought changing your name. Rosa and Lazar are thinking abought it also, though Lazars business is doing well here. Which you must be aware of. Mother is well. I am sufring from indigestion. Dont wright abought it in your next letter, Mother would worry, I can put up with it. I almost forgot the main pupose of this leter I am having to take out life insurance for the Bond. It is very expensiv for me so I am taking it out in your name if you dont object. I am saving money that way. The weather was very bad lately, it was always raining. If I suceed with my building things will be allright. We send you and your wife our greeting and hope if things work out we will see you again one day.

Your Loving Father,

I. Dunsky

Max

Pretoria, 1929

Look, when I came to this country I didn't know a bull from a cow, now I can put my arm inside a carcass find the liver, the spleen, the honeycomb, the biblebags. Right in, up to the shoulder, covered in blood. If you are willing to get your hands dirty not keep your nose in books this country has every promise you could want. How a man can worry himself to death about what is happening to strangers in some place he has never been half way around the world I do not understand. Whatever a man can want is here.

Let me tell you when I got off the boat and rode the train for three days through all that empty land my heart was thumping in my chest with the possibilities. In Riga you had to use every trick to make a kopek. You had to fight for every piece of business, cut your margins to nothing, and from that nothing you had to pay the tax man, the inspector, the police, every gonef sitting in an office with his name on the door. Here when I came you didn't even have to pay to get a contract, all I had to do was quote lower than the previous supplier, the little something I put in the handshake was money thrown away. Not that it mattered with the profits I was making. They were taking so much gold from the ground there was riches enough to go around. You know what killed my father? The tax man who had bled him dry said he had to pay another thousand rubles. A thousand rubles to a man who had never held that much money in his hand. You can understand a shock like that killing a man. Now I can spend a thousand rubles and not even notice it.

The problem here is not the government or the tax man it's the workers. Back home people knew what it meant to keep a job. It was nothing to work fourteen hours a day. During the week you worked, on the Sabbath you rested. Nobody came in late drunk to work on a weekday. It's something Israel never properly understood. He didn't spend enough time on the floor, he was always in his office doing the books. Making the numbers meet while the workers were stealing behind his back. Kaffirs, whites, Jews, they're all the same, a few you can trust, the rest are no-good lazy trombeniks. You've got to be on their backs all the time or they'll verneuk you or spoil your meat with their stupidity. You get a cow excited before it's slaughtered it won't bleed properly, the flesh will be ruined. For twenty-four, thirty-six hours the animal's got to be kept calm and rested. Give it plenty of water but no food unless you want to cut it open and find a belly-load of kuck. From a rested animal the hide comes away better too, the pustunpasniks can't spoil it so easily. It's a business, I'm in it to make money. You think I wanted to be a butcher? To come home every night to my wife's bed stinking of animal meat? Blood under my finger-nails and in my hair? It's a business, to make a life for myself, for my family. If some thief is ruining my goods, I am going to keep him on my payroll?

You want to know something? When I got to Germiston and I saw the little grocery store with the house behind, the roof held down by stones on each corner, I didn't know whether to laugh or cry. All I ever heard at home was Israel the genius, Israel the rabbi, how the whole world would know Israel, how Israel would save our family. Every day I was told I was nothing compared to this Israel. Once or twice a year a pale thin young man I barely knew would come home for a week or two, spend most of his time read-ing books, smoke a few cigarettes, then go again and we wouldn't see him until the next holidays. If he said two words to me I thought I had been blessed. The last time I saw him before I came to Germiston was ten years earlier riding away on a cart like a prince leaving his kingdom, my mother weeping, my father staring after him until he was a speck in the distance. And now here he was, this genius, standing behind the counter of this little store like some store from home with a few tins and sacks on the shelves, counting his pennies. Do you know what he wanted me to do? Sit in a corner giving shaves and cutting hair. People coming in to buy groceries will stop to have a shave and people coming for a hair cut will buy groceries, he said, like this was some big business idea that was going to make us all rich. Every time I saw him for five years after Dunsky Brothers was established I told him to come and work for me, but the truth is he liked that little store. He could sit there and read his Jewish books and journals in peace between customers. The bookworms would all come to sit around talking with him, drinking tea and putting their pennies in his little blue box. On Sundays he would go to play chess and meet with the other Zionists at the Jewish boarding house. He was happy, it was Pearl who couldn't stand it.

Make him a partner she kept telling me. If I had made him partner none of us would have had any money. He'd have given it all to the Jewish homeland or lost it on one of his big business ideas. Every time I saw him he had a different one. Ostrich feathers, delivering milk, Jewish bakers, kosher soap. The best ones never got further than the talking, at least he didn't lose any money on them. Sell the store, I'll pay you every month what it earns you in a year, I told him. I didn't like to see them in that farkuckt hut, Pearl having to cook on a brick stove even if she always looked down her long nose at me. Still does, even after everything I've done for them. When she complained Rosa had nowhere to practise piano I went straight out and bought a Bechstein for her. You think the best manager I could find for Pretoria was a man who had lost all his money on opening a bioscope in a town that was dying from the diggings drying up ? It's true he learned in time, he got better at business. He made a go of his own meat business, though of course it wasn't worth half what I paid him for it. I wanted to make him and his family financially secure once and for all. And what did he do? Took out the life insurance policy for his building on Eli instead of himself just to save a few stupid pounds.

He couldn't see what was in front of his own nose that was his problem. Talking all the time about the Land of Israel when there is so much land here they have put aside an area the size of Palestine just for animals. If you want to dig up water and plant fruit trees in the desert you can do it here, in this desert, only this desert is fertile, it's got water, it isn't owned by the Sultan of Turkey. Forget the vineyards of Engedi, they got vineyards here that make better wine than anything from Palestine. So it says in the Bible that God gave that land to the Jews, you don't have to tell me what it says in the Bible, I wasted ten years of my life studying the Bible in that dark little heder, and most of it is rubbish.

If he didn't forget what really matters maybe he wouldn't have got himself into such a state over these happenings in

Hebron. I'm not saying it's not a tragedy. I am a Jew. I do not like it when Arabs creep into a Jewish village in the night and slaughter a hundred defenceless women and children. But what good did it do them that Israel stayed up all night to write a speech and then went out in the rain to deliver it to the meeting when the doctor told him to rest. What can you expect of Palestine? It's in the Bible, everyone killing each other, Jews, Canaanites, Arabs, Philistines, fighting, making war. It's what I always tried to tell him. This is the Promised Land. This land. No one's going to murder people in their beds here. The Kaffirs are happy that the white people are here to employ them, to run the country, to build up this land. Like what happened at the funeral. I looked up in the middle of the speeches, I saw twenty Kaffirs standing outside the fence staring into the cemetery at us. I was about to wave them away when I recognized them for Dunsky Brothers workers and saw the tears on some of their cheeks, so I let them stay.

Queens

London & Frinton-on-Sea, 1938

What are you doing with your mouth, Israel? I hope you are not making fun of Nanny's dentures again. You're not so perfect yourself, you know, with those sticking out ears and that nose which I can tell you has been growing again.

Israel, come here and help me with my wool. Don't make that face at me, I've got to get Mrs Adler's order done by Thursday. What have you got to do except laze around getting in the way and teasing poor Ruthie?

Well you can go out when I've done this, I'll be glad to get a little peace in the house.

Keep your hands up.

Stop scowling, you think I'm doing this for pleasure? Where do you think the money comes from to put food on the table and clothes on your back? Do you want to go without your supper tonight? Well then.

Oh I'm just sitting here reading the Jewish Chronicle. They're going on about the German boycott again, as if any self-respecting Jew is still buying German.

What gloves?

I think that's very unfair of you, Zelda. That was last winter. Not all of us can afford English calfskin and you know how sensitive my hands are to cold.

Oh, nothing much. There's the new Muni film which I want to see and apparently now the Czechs have started up an anti-Jewish drive. It really is too awful to read about, we are so fortunate to be here. My heart bleeds for the Jews in Europe. I would boycott Czech too, if they made anything worth boycotting.

I'd better have two pairs of the shorts please and two ties. For the West London Jewish Day School. I don't know what he does to them. Chews them or wipes his nose on them.

What's the matter with you Israel? You wouldn't make that face if you knew how ugly you look.

Nonsense. They've just got room for you to grow into.

Who says that?

Well you can tell him that not every boy's mother can afford to buy her son new shorts every term.

You should have seen his little face when he looked in the mirror. The last time I bought him new shorts apparently Alex Silverleaf, the little leech, said he couldn't tell whether they were long shorts or short longs. Oh Zelda, I did feel rather guilty, they are rather large, he looked so crestfallen. It was all I could do to keep a straight face, but it's not my fault if every time I buy him new clothes he grows three inches in a week. I made it up to him though, I took him to Herzog's and let him choose the biggest bar of chocolate in the shop.

It's me, I just got back from Mrs Adler's, she was all over my creations, she says they are the smartest in town, can you believe it? She wants two dozen more by the end of the month, I am going to have to get some help and work even harder. I only hope Eli isn't going to make a fuss.

Israel, I want you to sit down now and write that letter to your Uncle Boris.

Because he's your uncle, that's why. He's your uncle and he wrote to us and he's not getting any younger and he hasn't got any of his own children. And don't forget to sign it Israel Dunsky not Dunn. It won't do any harm to remind him whose grandson you are.

Well if that's the way you feel I don't know why you married me. You knew I would never be the perfect little housewife, counting pennies and stretching the leftovers all week. I knew what I was getting with you and I don't complain. It's not easy keeping this house on seven hundred pounds a year especially with a sister who has no money worries at all. If the Gas Light & Coke Company were to give you that pay rise you keep talking about then I wouldn't have to do my knitting. I don't want to work my fingers to the bone and go around hawking my creations like some poor peddler to Mrs Adler and Diana Goddess of Sport. I'm only trying to earn myself a little pin money so I can buy the occasional dress or pair of shoes to look nice for you.

Oh Zelda, it was awful. He was absolutely beastly to me, shouting and criticizing me. He said I am never there for him or the children, it's already making me lose my looks, it's only because I'm so extravagant, most wives could manage perfectly well on the money he earns. Well I wasn't going to put up with that and I fought back as best I could, he got angrier and angrier, all red in the face with that vein on his head looking as if it was really going to burst this time, eventually he stormed out of the door slamming it behind him. I sat there with tears streaming down my face. My only consolation was the thought that if he really had left me I would start up my own proper business and make something of my creations, I was beginning to cheer up when he returned. He was all sorry, bending down in front of me and putting his head in my lap and apologizing and saying he was a fool and he loved me and I could knit as many jumpers as I liked. I told him I didn't want to knit, that if I could only get enough orders I could get someone else to do that and I'd concentrate on the sales and design. Well, the upshot is I'm going to do Mrs Adler's order and I'm going back to Diana Goddess of Sport on Tuesday week.

Israel, if you are responsible for what Nanny has just found floating in the toilet you are in big trouble.

It's not funny, Eli. His personality is too strong for me to control. Poor Nanny had to take to her bed and I had to look after Ruthie. I barely got a stitch of work done all day.

Well who else would have put Nanny's senna pods in the toilet? Nanny was in a terrible state, she hasn't had a movement since Wednesday anyway.

I really don't think it's something to laugh about. Just because your problems are the opposite.

—

163

I told you, Zelda, we finally went to see Muni as Emile Zola. He was even better than in Louis Pasteur. If he doesn't win the Academy Award again it'll be a scandal. The only bad part was Eli drooling over the females, though of course he denied it. That and having to sit through the newsreel from Vienna. It was quite chilling watching the horrible little man standing there with his arm in the air while the thousands marched past. I have to say that moustache really is ridiculous, I don't know how the Germans can put up with him.

What's the matter with the bicycle you've got?

Well don't bend your knees so much and they won't hit the handlebars.

I don't care what your cousins have. And don't let me hear you talking like that in front of your father. He works very hard to make a living for this family and a good living compared to most people. Uncle Victor may make more money than your father, but I can tell you I wouldn't swap Eli for a hundred Victor Fondlers and you wouldn't either. So you be careful what you say young man, do you hear me?

I wasn't gossiping, Eli, I was talking to Zelda about the Austrian girl she's sponsoring. Apparently she's a brilliant cellist but the only way they can get her out is by claiming she's going to work for them as a maid. It's no problem getting her out of Austria, it's getting her into this country that's like breaking into Fort Knox. I would sponsor one myself if we had any room but with Nanny in with Ruthie already and Israel in the boxroom I don't think it's fair to take someone when you can't provide for them properly.

I've just had Betty Noyk on the telephone, she's been to see the Modigliani at Tooth's Gallery. We must go and see it, apparently he's even better than da Vinsky.

Israel? Come here. Your school report has arrived.

Yes, you should look ashamed. Just wait until your father reads this. Untidy, disinclined to listen, argumentative. At least he will have to realize I haven't been making it up about your personality. I dread to think what will become of you. With your looks and lack of brains you'll have to be a chef, at least that way you'll eat.

It's not true, Eli, I try my best to love him, it's just he's so difficult whereas Ruthie I find so charming. He always has such ready answers for everything and such a smug expression while Ruthie has a gentle dreamy personality like me. Anyway it's the same with you. You like Israel better than you like Ruthie, you always have.

Of course it's true, Eli. In all families there are favourites, it's only human.

Why are you looking at me like that?

I think I'm going to start fining Eli for shouting at me too, Zelda. He can't afford twenty-five pounds a quarrel like you charge Victor but I've decided a guinea is reasonable. It should make him think twice and that way if he still wants to be horrible to me I can buy myself a little something as consolation.

Don't talk to me about the Jewish Problem. I've got two Jewish Problems in my house. The two dictators, Hitler and Mussolini, I call them.

Listen Zelda I need to talk to you, I've just come back from Diana Goddess of Sport. Madam Adele loved my jumpers. She couldn't believe I designed them myself. She's ordered a dozen and a dozen more if they go. Anyway that wasn't what I wanted to tell you. She says I'm wasted on jumpers and I should be doing frocks. Of course she can't help me but I started thinking and I suddenly thought why don't I do some designs for Victor. I was racking my brains and all along my own brother-in-law makes frocks. I know what he makes is rather different but what do you think? Will you talk to him about it? I'm very excited about this idea.

–

Where have you been, Israel?

That's very peculiar because I just had a telephone call from Mrs Noyk and she was saying how nice it was to see you and Ezra Harris and Montgomery Cohen at the service for Shavuot, even if you weren't dressed properly.

Oh, is that right?

And did you find the service interesting?

Well then, I'll have to talk to your father about you attending shul on a more regular basis.

It was hilarious, Zelda, you know they had that flood at the shul, apparently they rented the Odeon at the last minute for Shavuot, like they do with the overflow service at Yom Kippur. Anyway Israel and his little chums obviously didn't realize, they must have snuck in the back entrance expecting to get into Tarzan for free, instead they got one of Rabbi Jacobson's marathons. They couldn't leave, they had to stay for the whole thing. You should have seen his little face when I confronted him with it.

I know I'm only supposed to telephone you at work in an emergency but this is an emergency. Oh, Eli, it's awful, Victor has rejected my designs. He says I don't have a feel for the market, can you believe that? My creations are good enough for Diana Goddess of Sport but not for Vizelda.

I know I shouldn't, but I was so hoping he would take them on, I'm never going to make more than the odd pound with my knitting, I thought if Victor would do some of my designs I could make a little money. He was so dismissive you would think I am just some little person off the street not his wife's sister who has already had some considerable success d'estime at the top end of the business.

She was no help at all, defending him when all I hear from her is how horrible he is to her. It's lucky she doesn't know the half of it, though with that red face, bald pate and heavy clumsy body I can't imagine why any woman would let him near them. Have you ever noticed how the tip of his nose is always wet? Oh Eli, I don't know what to do. I am getting old and grey and whatever I do seems to be foolish.

Freud in London? Good, I can send the Jewish Problems to see him.

It's me, Eli's taken the children to the beach so I thought I'd treat myself to a trunk call and see if you were back from France. I've had to wait an hour to get through.

It's Frinton, what do you expect? If we were staying at the White House Hotel it might be different, but Mrs Frankel's is Mrs Frankel's. At least the weather's nice, we've been spending every day on the beach. Eli is so relaxed, the sun's burned him as black as a darkie and his eyes are glistening. We went out last night, it was like old times. It makes me realize how much work takes out of him and what a sacrifice he made to marry me. If he hadn't met me he could have finished his studies and become a proper scientist like he always dreamed, maybe he would have been the next Einstein.

Zelda, it's me again, I can't talk long, it took me ages to get through and the children are waiting to go for lunch.

No, Eli's back in London, I've stayed on with the children. To tell you the truth, it's a relief he's gone, I couldn't bear him seeing me on the beach looking like a frump next to all the beauties. The first time I put on my costume I looked down and got a terrible shock. Not that Eli said anything, he thinks my squat little body is perfect.

Of course we're glued to the radio, I'm keeping my fingers crossed for Mr Chamberlain. When Eli got home he found a telegram from South Africa, it was Rosa begging us to go to South Africa but I find it too far away being here.

Your guess is as good as mine, we're stuck here until it goes one way or the other. I even went to see a school down here for Israel in case it goes on much longer. It's not Jewish of course and it's boarding, but I can't handle him myself for much longer.

He's optimistic but I don't know. I'm definitely fasting for Yom Kippur this year to keep on the right side of God. Plus I really must lose a little weight.

It's me, Zelda, we're back, thank God. Another week in Frinton with the children and I would have gone mad.

Well, Eli's not so optimistic, but I had it on the best advice that it was all bluff anyway. This man I met assured me that Germany couldn't possibly afford a war, in two months they would have no food left and not enough iron to make a single battery. Or was it bullet? I can't remember.

By the way there was a shop down there selling very nice leather bags, I got one for myself and one for you. I'm sure you'll like it. I bought them for gas masks but they're perfect for anything really.

1 Soldiers

c/o G (C.W.) Branch, British Troops

4 July 1940

Dearest Golda,

Cheer up and do not be despondent. I think that you are in a fairly safe spot and so is Israel. Be assured that England cannot lose this war and I am one of those who believe we will win it sooner rather than later. Then we will all be back to normal. I am sorry for you that Victor seems to be a permanency in Amersham but it is he who is renting the cottage and has taken you and Ruthie in so I don't think you can complain. At least you are with Zelda and between the two of you I am sure you can deal with him.

It is a pity that Israel's school had to move so far away but they could not have stayed in Frinton and at least the Welsh coast is as safe from Hitler as possible. I got Israel's first letter from Wales which you sent on. It sounds a most interesting place. I think he is very lucky to be going to a school in a castle with suits of armour and a cellar and beaches and fields nearby. Visits may be a problem in term-time but there are the holidays. I will write to Mr. Gimley about getting one of the masters who lives in London to bring him on the train when the term ends, and you can meet him there. Hopefully, I will be able to spend some time with you all then.

I don't think you should worry too much about this name business, and I think we should write to him as Jack. It upsets me too, Israel after all was my father's name, and one which he treasured and would never have changed for anything. But don't forget I changed our surname and the reasons for doing so. Israel is the only Jew in a Christian school and Mr. Gimley's reasons for giving him a new name were to avoid him being teased and singled out. It is the same reason why we agreed to him going to daily chapel. I think Mr. Gimley was quite sensitive to choose Jack which you seem to have forgotten is a shortening of Jacob which is another name for Israel in the Bible. Of course we don't want him to forget his real name or who he is. Don't worry, I will have a good talk with him about all this when I see him.

I am trying to find out when I can get some leave or if I am going to be moved to somewhere permanent where you can come and see me. I am missing you very much, and little Ruthie too. Would you please send me my trench-coat lining and also my scarf. It gets very chilly here in the evenings and the fleece lining would be useful as a dressing jacket when reading in my room at night.

With heaps of love to you and Ruthie,

Eli

14 Nov 1940

Dearest Golda,

I am now on board ship though I do not know when we will be leaving. The ship is a luxurious one and I have an excellent cabin, which I share with two others. How I should have enjoyed this journey if made with you and the children on a different errand. Still Nazism must be wiped out and we have to make our little sacrifice in common with others.

At least we have seen each other before I leave. It was a wonderful weekend and I shall cherish it in the times ahead. Of course I will write to Israel but you must make sure he realizes how sorry I am not to have had a chance to say goodbye to him. In some ways perhaps it is easier for him though I would have loved to have seen his impish little face. I did also want to have a talk with him about his remark about chapel, and remind him that there is a little more difference between Judaism and Christianity than that they sit down and take their hats off to pray while we stand up and put ours on.

I will write to him about behaving himself and washing and cleaning his teeth and everything without being told when he comes to Amersham, but please remember not to nag him too much. He is a ten-year-old boy and cannot be controlled as easily as a little girl. I am enclosing a passport photograph that was taken in my captain's uniform. It is not very good but it is all I have to give to Israel and would you send it to him for me. One good thing about my going away is I will be able to get some exotic stamps for his new collection. Tell Ruthie I loved her sweet little drawings and letter. I will make sure I send her a letter of her own before we sail.

Au revoir, my darling, I shall always think of you and shall be looking forward eagerly to our reunion.

Yours as ever,

Eli

24 Dec 1940

Dearest Golda,

In my last letter I wrote that we were heading for a certain place. Well, we have been there and I have had a very moving and special time. Immediately on getting ashore I put a trunk call through to Rosa, as my people had no idea I was coming and I didn't want to give Mother a shock. I waited on tenterhooks for one-and-a-half hours before being connected. Then a strange sounding voice answered.

It is fifteen years since I have spoken to my sister and you will understand if it was a very emotional conversation for both of us. Well she said immediately that she would come to see me and the next evening she and Mother arrived together.

I recognized Rosa at once and of course Mother also. Rosa is very plump and rather nervous, but very talkative and likeable and in time I felt that I was back with my sister once again. Mother is very well though she has let her hair go completely grey since her visit to England. She still looks attractive and not her age. We immediately went along to a hotel where they put up and then started talking. We talked of old times, of you and the children, of Lazar, my relations, Rosa's little ones. I would have loved to have seen the children but I am glad really she did not bring them so we could talk properly. Everyone is well here, my uncles included, and they are very sad you did not decide to come here. Lazar's business is still doing well though he has not become the great artistic photographer that he thinks he should have been. I think financially Mother is now fine, so you will be pleased we do not have to worry about supporting her.

I was so contented, you cannot imagine, and did not envy at all the others their fun and games. All I wanted was a quiet corner where we could chat together. We went swimming every day. Mother is still madly fond of bathing. The sea was very strong, even I had difficulty in standing up to the waves, but Mother went in two or three times daily. It was very sad when my last day came and we had to say goodbye. We went and took some photographs of me in uniform and I sent a print with them for Uncle Boris who apparently requested one, which I was pleasantly surprised to hear. I am sending one for you and one to send on to Israel.

After so much excitement it is rather a let down to be back at sea. The sea is extremely smooth like polished metal. Later today there is a Hanukah service on board which I think I shall go along to. I have come across one other Jewish officer and I think there is a second and a number of men.

I hope you are enjoying your holidays together, though of course by the time this letter reaches you they will be long over. I hate being away from you but keep thinking of the future when we shall be together again. I love and adore you my darling. God bless you and the children.

Your adoring and devoted husband,

Eli

16 Mar 1941

My dearest Golda,

What joy this morning when your first letters finally caught up with me. I went to the post as usual but instead of returning empty-handed I marched back triumphantly with a whole pile of letters dating right up almost to Xmas. I would not speak to anyone and lay down on my bed to read them and when I had done so I read them all again, though I must say it has made me rather homesick, or more correctly sick for the sight and touch of you. I would be happy enough if you could come to me where I am.

After the war I should like to bring you to this place to show you all its sights and bask with you in its wonderful climate. The surroundings are very beautiful and the nearby village most picturesque. It is most cruel of the Germans to ravage the peaceful countryside and drive innocent villagers from their homes. This morning when the village bells sounded the air-raid alarm two little tots who were away from their homes cowered against a wall. It made my blood boil, especially with what you wrote about little Ruthie worrying about me. She is such a sensitive girl and must not be allowed to upset herself. I cannot bear to think of her crying herself to sleep at night. A much happier image is of her trooping off to school, and I shall think of that instead.

I am very sorry to hear that Israel did not make it home for the holidays. I am sure you tried your very best to find a way for him to do so, but it seems hard to believe that none of the masters could have brought him up to London. Of course it is easy for me to say that from here. I was pleased to get Israel's letters that you sent on though do you not find them rather disappointing? The only adjective he seems to use is 'super'. And the letters have so little about him. I am pleased he has friends but I do not want to hear only about Simpson, Halliday and Tippers (can that be his real name?) Israel not Tippers is our son after all.

I am sorry to hear that he does not think I am a proper soldier because I have not killed any Germans yet. I wonder how many fathers of boys in his school have, though I would not shy from the chance. I get more bloodthirsty every day and would love to give the Germans and Italians hell.

I would not worry about him playing rugby. It is a good sport, I played it and never did myself any serious damage. Of course he must not neglect his studies. The fees were reduced in the expectation that he would get a scholarship and though that time is still a long way away, what he does now will lay the foundations for the work ahead. I have been sending him lots of stamps and I hope he has received them.

I was very pleased to hear that Victor is making his contribution to the war effort. I would love to have seen his face when he received notice that he had to give over his factory to the production of service underwear. God help all the Waacs if he decides he needs to do some 'research'. I am assuming that this letter will not be read by Zelda.

My darling, it has been wonderful to hear in my head

your familiar chirpy voice and to know you are well and not too unhappy. Things may look black at the moment but keep cheerful. Nobody here is at all depressed about the recent reverses and everyone is confident of the future. I often dream of we two enjoying a happy and delightful middle age observing our two fine children growing up. I hope that will come to pass and we will all four of our little family join in building a better country together.

I send you all my love,

Eli

8 June 1941

My darling Golda,

If I have not written to you for the last few weeks it is not because you have not been in my thoughts, but because things have been difficult about postage and so on. You see I have been through the famous Cretan campaign, in which I turned fighting soldier, though please don't worry as I am now in a safe spot. I am getting over an attack of dysentery and a twisted ankle, my sole wounds of the campaign. I am being well cared for and am happily resting up.

I must say I had an experience and you can tell Israel that his father has seen quite a bit of action. I did not kill any Germans, not knowingly at least, but I shouldered a rifle and took charge of about 30 men. We rounded up parachutists, manned part of a line and were blitzed from the air for nearly 12 hours a day. It was quite something to see the Germans drop from the sky. The ones we captured were not bad fellows actually. They tried their best not to be captured, but once we had them they were very sporting and accepted their situation like gentlemen. Of course you know the outcome. The withdrawal was very hard, marching mile after mile to the point of evacuation, being chased by the Jerry planes all the way. It was very frightening but actually casualties from air attacks are low provided you take elementary precautions. We marched only at night and dug in during the day. Ordinary trenches afford marvellous protection. It was the thought of you, and how you would suffer if I was taken prisoner, that kept me going and gave me fresh determination when I was already suffering from the stomach troubles and having to hobble quite badly because of my ankle.

The Navy did a wonderful job getting us all away, or all who made it to the evacuation point. Quite a few were left behind. I was sorry to leave Crete, I had grown very fond of the people and the country and it is a great pity the Hun should be in possession. By the way, the only thing of my personal possessions I saved apart from what I was wearing were your letters which I kept stuffed down my shirt and the scarf you knitted me – I clung to that for dear life.

I will be here for a little while longer until I am fully recovered and then will be moving on. It may be I will get a chance to go to a certain place my father always dreamed about going to. I have had no more of your letters since the first batch but I have made inquiries. Do not worry. Despite our setbacks here the RAF are performing wonders in the home skies and over Northern France.

Keep well, my darling. Give my regards to Victor and Zelda and my love to little Ruthie.

Yours as ever,

Eli

17 July 1941

Dearest Golda,

I have been here nearly two weeks and as I don't know how much longer I will stay I am making the most of my time. I have been to Jerusalem and walked all round Tel Aviv and they are both most interesting towns in very different ways. I have been thinking a lot about my father and wondering why he did not at least visit here on holiday. There were various points in his life when he could have afforded the time and money but I suppose he did not want to come lightly but to wait until he was in a position to fulfil his dreams. It does seem a pity though that he never saw this place for it is a very beautiful and fascinating country. Perhaps if I am still in this region when the war ends you might find a way to come out and spend a couple of months here with me.

Last night I went to an open air concert given by the Palestine Orchestra and I enjoyed it thoroughly. Though small, they are really excellent. The moon was shining and the garden was covered by trees. The sound of the violins appeared to come from the leaves. The whole effect was really quite magical. Earlier in the week I had to go out of town for some work. At the end of the day I found myself stuck without anywhere to sleep or have supper. I had a brainwave of going into the synagogue to the service and afterwards I had a choice of a dozen homes to go to. I was eventually taken home by the Rabbi. He was a very nice man with two rather pretty young daughters. Supper was very pleasant and the next morning I went on my way well-fed and happy.

I hope you have made arrangements for Israel's Hebrew lessons over the holidays. His barmitzvah is not very far away now and he will only be able to study Hebrew in the holidays, so he really must work at it then. Of course I fully expect to be back with you by that time. I received your letter about the cricket gear and I fully agree with you. I will write to Israel about it. The school provides pads, gloves, bats and so on for the very reason that they are expensive and the boys grow out of them quickly. If he continues to practise hard and do well in the team then maybe next season we can reconsider, especially about the bat. By the time you get this term will have ended anyway and you will all be together for the holidays. I hope you will all be having a very happy time together. I am sure Ruthie will be delighted to have her brother back home with her and to have some male influence. It is one thing to be sensitive and idealistic as you call her, another to be afraid of the rough and tumble of life. Or does that sound a bit harsh? It is so difficult for me so far away. I am sure you will do what is best.

I send my love to all three of you.

Yours as ever,

Eli

21 Sept 1941

Dear Golda,

I have just received a letter from you and I have to say I almost wish I hadn't. It is quite unthoughtful and pointed towards me when I have done nothing wrong and not said the things you are accusing me of. For a start let me tell you that the Rabbi's daughters were eight and ten years old and the reason I mentioned them at all was because for the first time in nearly a year I had supper with a family and children and it made me think of my family and how wonderful they are and how much I am looking forward to seeing them all again. That was why I went away happy, not for the reasons you are insinuating which I must say are beneath you and quite unfair. I hope you will not make them again.

As to my 'threatening' as you call it to move you out to Palestine after the war, I never said any such thing. I merely wrote that it is a beautiful place and I would love to travel around it in better times with you. How you turned that into a threat I don't know. I would never make you and the children come to a dangerous place nor 'tear' you away from your beloved sister. I am fully aware that things are not likely to be easy here when the war ends. As it happens I can tell you I am not so enamoured of this place as you seem to think, especially since I have acquired an internal tenant in the form of a tapeworm here. I was very shocked to discover this as you can imagine and immediately shot into hospital and was starved for 48 hours. Then I took large doses of a horrible medicine which turfed the visitor out. That was two days ago and I have been feeling rather strange ever since. I will not be too sorry to leave Palestine as I expect to do soon.

In truth I am thoroughly fed up with this whole part of the world with its heat and dust and people grabbing you all the time as you walk down the street. I long to come home to you and the children and England. Being away has made me appreciate what an attractive country it is and I can't wait to see its green fields again even if it is raining and misty. London also, with its curious mixture of good and bad, has got me and I doubt if I would like to live elsewhere.

I must also say that I object to your complaining about Israel too. What I would give to spend a summer in Amersham with Israel and Ruth. I do not doubt that he ran you a little ragged with his energy and his cheek but that is only his strong and lively character. As to his 'social faults', well there are relatives on both sides of the family from whom he might have inherited these. He is a stubborn and determined little fellow and most of that should be encouraged. I am sorry if I am sounding cross but you do make me so with a letter like this. At first I was very pleased to see how much you had written but as I read it all seemed to be complaints and attacks, though I was very moved by your description of Israel's arrival home and his first day.

You can give my thanks to Victor for buying Israel the cricket gear though I hope Israel did not ask for it and I must say it does annoy me after I said no. I would like to think that when a boy's father rules something other members of his family would respect that decision. I only wish I could have been there to go to the shop with Israel. Now that he has got his kit I expect him to look after it properly. He should whiten the pads regularly and make sure he keeps the willow supple with oil, preferably linseed. I will write to him about this.

Yours as ever,
Eli

7 *May 1942*

Dearest Golda,

I have just received a couple of letters and the snaps and they will take their place in the little gallery which I often look at to revive my spirits. Israel's puckish bright-eyed little face and Ruthie so pretty with her hair in curls. You look amazingly young, just like a schoolgirl yourself, and much too attractive to be let loose as a waitress on all those soldiers. I am quite jealous even thinking about it and I hope you are being good. Wouldn't it be wonderful if I could stroll one day into your Naafi, just casually sit down and ask for a tea and a bun. Would you drop your tray? You must write and tell me about all your experiences there.

I am very pleased you went to see Israel at school and I am grateful again to Victor for taking you there in the car even if I am jealous that it was not me. I wonder where Victor got so much petrol? I am sure he could not have got it all on rations. But I suppose I should not ask. It sounds like you had a very nice time of it, though I was rather surprised to read that you spent half your afternoon with Israel in the ladieswear shops in the town. Was that really necessary? Could you not have taken Israel for a picnic or to the pictures or somewhere nice for tea? I appreciate Victor standing in for me but I hope Israel is not too influenced by him. Money and women's fashion are not the only important things.

For example, school. You do not say whether Israel has been working hard. I will be interested to see his report. His scholarship exams are coming up and he must take them very seriously. I will remind him when I write next that he cannot do as his pals do as they may not need to win scholarships. A good scholarship will set him up for his life ahead.

I am thinking about buying him a watch for his barmitzvah so please do not let anyone else do that. I would like you to tell Victor particularly as I don't want Israel getting two watches. I will have a look at the watches next time I go into town, though I may be leaving Syria soon so perhaps I should wait and see where I end up. Where that might be I don't know. Of course I hope home but it seems unlikely. I am hopeful however that I will be home for Israel's barmitzvah. I must certainly not miss that.

It is a year and a half since we have seen each other and I wonder how it will be when we see each other again.

I remain your loving husband,

Eli

25 Dec 1942

My dear Golda,

It is Xmas morning and I am alone in the office. I offered to hold the fort today so that the others could enjoy their festival. We gave all our staff, including the Indian clerks and orderlies presents for Xmas. Yesterday evening when I came in I found the office specially cleaned up, my desk with new blotting paper and flowers on it and the smell of incense, all looking very cosy and pleasant. The Indian orderly had done it. Later one of the Indian clerks came in with a huge bunch of flowers and some oranges, it was quite touching.

I am afraid that we will have to accept now that I will not be there with you for Israel's barmitzvah. I hate the thought of it but can do nothing. I will write to Victor to ask him to take my place. You can be sure I will be thinking of you all and hoping it will not be too much longer before you can tell me about it face to face, though of course you must write to me all about it. I cannot bear that I am missing so much of our children's growing up. When I come back I will make it up to Israel and to Ruthie for these long years apart.

I have bought a watch for Israel and will send it to you in the next few days to keep for his special day. It turns out these things are more expensive in Baghdad than they would have been where I was before, but that is how it goes. It is the same make as mine, but waterproof, and with a large second hand which should delight Israel. I believe such watches are very valuable in England today, so you should consider insuring it. I hope having this watch will help to make Israel increase his sense of responsibility

Even from afar it brings me great comfort to know that Israel is having a barmitzvah. I have been quite depressed at what I have been reading about the Jews in Europe. It is hard to know what exactly is going on but it seems many of them are suffering quite badly, though I suppose that is true of most people. I was annoyed that by the time I heard about the day of fasting and mourning announced by the Chief Rabbi it had already passed. I will do my own little fast when I can in the next day or two. I have been wondering about my cousins on my father's side in Riga. I do not think anyone has heard from them for some time, though of course since the Germans invaded the post will have been difficult.

My darling, soon this blasted war will be over and the world will be able to resume its normal existence.

I send all my love to you.

Yours as ever,

Eli

Esther

Riga, 1943

Proverbials

Wallstone School, Hampshire

Christian *adj.* Human; civilized, decent, respectable.
> *Oxford Shorter English Dictionary, third edition, 1944*

Jew *v. colloq.* To cheat or overreach.
> *Oxford Shorter English Dictionary, third edition, 1944*

"'Ow did you know I was English?"

"I make a practise," Mr Opie said with a smile, "of always thinking the best of people."
> Graham Greene, *Stamboul Train*, 1932

"Look through there in the first class, Amy. Can't you see her? Too good for us, that's what she is."

"With that Jew? Well, one knows what to think."
> Graham Greene, *Stamboul Train*, 1932

His head was singing like a burst kettle: his back felt as if it was broken where a vast lump of ceiling had hit him. But after moving his legs and then his arms he decided that he was still alive. And having arrived at that moment's conclusion the necessity for prompt action became evident.

Sapper, *The Black Gang*, 1922

"Fetch the cat."

In silence one of the men left the room, and as his full meaning came home to the two Jews they flung themselves grovelling on the floor, screaming for mercy.

Sapper, *The Black Gang*, 1922

His host was called Warriner, a fine, old, high-coloured sportsman, who looked as if his winters had been spent in the hunting-field, and his summers in trampling his paternal acres. He was a fantastic old gentleman, for he directed all his conversation to Adam, and engaged him in a discussion on Norse remains in Britain.

John Buchan, *A Prince of Captivity*, 1933

Mr Mcandrew's name was misleading, for he was clearly a Jew, a small man with a nervous mouth and eyes that preferred to look downward. He seemed to have been expecting Adam for he cut short his explanation. "Yes, yes, yes," he said.

John Buchan, *A Prince of Captivity*, 1933

What pulled Scott through was character, sheer good grain.

Apsley Cherry-Garrard, *The Worst Journey in the World*,
1922

The truth was that Amundsen was an explorer of the markedly intellectual type, rather Jewish than Scandinavian.

Apsley Cherry-Garrard, *The Worst Journey in the World*,
1922

Ruggles got up to open the door for Dr. Richmond. Yes, Dr. Richmond might be the smartest student St. Martha's had known for many years, but he wasn't smug. He had a joke and a smile for you, what's more he was a comely lad, straight in the back and thick in the shoulders, a little stocky perhaps for his height, which was five feet nine. He was black of hair and fresh of face, clear cut, and steady and blue of eye, the sort of man who would not flinch in a tight corner.

Warwick Deeping, *The Dark House*, 1941

Ruggles got out of his box with his teeth showing in his beard. He tiptoed to the door, and opened it suddenly and fiercely. The expected figure stood revealed on the doorstep. It wore a huge bowler hat, a long black overcoat almost down to its feet. It had a sallow face, and a hook nose, and a black retriever beard. It lisped.

"The doctor, pleath, mithter, at once, pleath."

It tendered a card, but Ruggles did not look at the card. He held a large fist close to the Hebraic nose.

"Here, you foot it, Moses. Shin off, and don't you show yer ruddy face 'ere for a week, or I'll smash it. Get out."

The Jew cringed and whimpered.

"But I vant the doctor, pleath. My wife –"

Ruggles put out a large hand on the creature's chest, and pushed him off the doorstep.

Warwick Deeping, *The Dark House*, 1941

Eric Lock, a tough little Shropshireman who had been with me at Hornchurch and collected twenty-three planes, a D.S.O., a D.F.C., and a bar: he had cannon-shell wounds in his arms and legs. On my left was Mark Mounsdon who trained with me in Scotland and was awaiting an operation on his eyelids. Beyond the partition was Joseph, the Czech sergeant pilot, also with a nose graft: Yorkey Law, a bombardier, blown up twice and burned at Dunkirk, with a complete new face taken in bacon strips from his legs, and no hands;

Richard Hillary, *The Last Enemy*, 1942

and Neft, a clever young Jew (disliked for it by the others), with a broken leg from a motor-cycle accident . . . and a tendency to complain, which caused Eric Lock to point out that some of us had been fighting the war with real bullets and would be infinitely grateful for his silence.

Richard Hillary, *The Last Enemy*, 1942

Diane turned in his arms and looked up at him with the tears running down her face. "I love you," she said, "please come back, Michael, please. I love you."

Manning Coles, *Drink to Yesterday*, 1940

Marie glanced up, caught sight of the Jew's hooked nose and pendulous lower lip in full profile, and looked hastily away again . . . "I am sorry – I have an engagement –"

Manning Coles, *Drink to Yesterday*, 1940

It was a little more than an hour ago that a grave and worrying message had dragged him from a comfortable dinner at his club; less than an hour since he had put through an official request to the B.B.C. for his carefully-worded SOS to be broadcast . . . In his job as Director of the newly-created Special Intelligence Branch of the Royal Air Force he could not afford to make mistakes. It was too costly; John Crispin had twenty-odd years of intelligence work behind him and he knew. In that mysterious calling they worked best who worked for the love of the game.

Richard Keverne, *The Black Cripple*, 1941

A swarthy, Jewish-looking man, with an untidy black beard, and so lame that he walked with the aid of two sticks, he was known in Berlin as an art dealer. But as Crispin had discovered, Carl Mendel had Hitler's ear; Carl Mendel was one of the few men, despite his obvious Jewish ancestry, whom the Fuhrer would always see . . . and Sir John had little doubt that the bearded German was chief organizer of the Nazi spy system in Britain.

Richard Keverne, *The Black Cripple*, 1941

2 Soldiers

Berlin, 1949

I know what I am talking about, I've been with all types, Amis, Ivans, the only type I've never gone with are Germans. I even had a Negro once. Don't look at me like that, I've got a class five red card, it's a starvation card, what do you want me to do, become a rubble lady and pass bricks along thank you please thank you please for seventy-two pfennigs an hour? How many calories is that going to get me? I could have got a better card by making up to some official but I told you I won't touch one of our own men, if you can call them men. I remember too well what they did for us when the Ivans came. I was down in the cellar with all our building, there'd been the bombing and shooting and after that silence. Then the door opened and a couple of Ivans peered in. They took the fat ones first, Ivans like them fat. Frau Hessler the butcher's wife was the fattest, as you can imagine, when they pulled her out she started squealing like a pig and what did her fat husband do to help her? Nothing. He just cowered in the corner whimpering. None of our men lifted a finger to help any of us. Some of them it was their own daughters being taken. It was my first time. First, second, third, fourth, and that was just that one day. That's why I like this frat I'm telling you about. I met him in Ronny's Bar. I was with this Ami boyfriend I'd been seeing for a few weeks, he was drunk as usual, and giving me a hard time because one of his friends said he'd seen me walking with someone else. He was shouting at me and holding my wrist so hard it hurt. I told him to let go but he wouldn't. That was when this Tommy walked over and asked if everything was alright, whether the lady needed any assistance. Lady he called me. It was like something out of a book. You don't get many Tommys in Ronny's and it was his voice as much as anything that surprised the Ami. You know that Tommy officer voice, he's not an officer, but he sounds like one, speaking so quietly but you can hear every word he says. He's not big but he looked that brute of an Ami right in the eye, and the Ami let go of my wrist and told him if he wanted to stick his nose in he could have me, it would serve him right when I did what I'd done to him. Then the Ami stood up and lurched off and left me with the Tommy. The funny thing was he didn't know what to say then, I had to take him in hand the rest of the evening. He hardly spoke a word all the way back to my flat and I had to do everything for him, take off his clothes, lie him down, show him where to put it. It's true what they say about the English being shy, though he's not cold. Afterwards he didn't go straight to sleep or leave as if he couldn't get away from me soon enough like some of them. He lay there and asked me about myself. It's the same even now, that's more than a month since Ronny's Bar. He doesn't jump on me the minute he comes in the door, or give me a few bars of chocolate and expect me to jump on him in return. He sits there and we talk though he doesn't like to hear about my other frats. I started telling him once, early on, he didn't say anything, but he went very quiet, and I knew he didn't like it. He likes me to talk about before the war, when I was young, what it was like in Germany then, and sometimes what my plans are for the future. I tell him who knows, it all depends, I don't tell him what I've started dreaming, this last month, since that evening in Ronny's Bar. His plan is to be a lawyer. He's going to university when he gets out of the army, he's got a place at that one, you know, the famous one. What he wants to be is a judge, that's his ambition, a judge making justice. He would be good at that, you can see it in his eyes, if I had to go in front of a judge I'd want it to be him. You know he'd be fair. Of course he doesn't give me as much as the Ami, Tommys don't have nylons and perfume falling out of their pockets like Amis, but he always brings me something, a few cigarettes or a bar of soap. He brought a real cotton sheet for the bed a few days ago and he's trying to get me some glass for the windows so I can take down some of the boarding and let in a little light. He's not so shy any more, but he's always gentle, and he only sometimes falls asleep afterwards. If he's got a hole in one of his socks I go and fetch it and sit in the bed darning it while he talks to me about cricket or books. I don't understand a word he says about cricket even though he's explained it a dozen times. He's trying to get me to read poetry, the other night he brought a book with him and read it to me in bed. It was so romantic, I didn't even listen to the poetry, I just watched his lips. He said there are some very good German poets, though not as good as the English ones. He was making a joke about that I think. Just when you think he's being the most serious you realize he's smiling. Not jokes about shit or piss like our men but little quiet jokes you can't understand. He always brings his own condoms, that's another thing. How do the Tommys say it? He's a proper English gentleman.

Leviticus

Oxford University, 1950–3

Are you Orthodox, Dunn?

Ah, Fairbairn then.

Fairbairn. If you're not Orthodox you must be Fairbairn.

Rowing, Dunn, that's what we're talking about aren't we? What style did you row at school, Orthodox or Fairbairn? Did you use fixed pins or swivels?

You didn't row at school? Well that's all right, old fellow, but why didn't you say so in the first place instead of going on about not being Orthodox?

*

The Livingstone Society is actually one of the oldest societies in the university and we get some rather distinguished speakers. If you are interested you really ought to come along to our first evening of the year, we've got a very good lady guest, Millicent Larchmont, she's just come back from travelling in the Soviet Union. It's a fascinating part of the world. Have you ever travelled there?

*

RUGGER CUPPERS

The Hall put up a brave fight but went out in the first round to Jesus by 27–3. The superior Jesus pack dominated and S. Leggett scored three tries from the wing with T. Light showing the form at fly half that will make him a contender for a Blue this year. E. S. Tanner stood out for the Hall and J. Dunn at scrum half displayed good spirit before being carried off injured half way through the second period.

Isis

*

Now it's interesting you should ask about that. I've been making a bit of a study of my predecessors the last few years, as it happens. In fact that reminds me, which one of you is Dunn again?

Ah yes, I should have known. I heard about you in the match. No damage done I hope.

Good, good. Now what we were talking about? Oh yes, I wanted to ask if you were related to the Dunn who was master here in the eighteen-thirties?

No? Are you sure? He was Scots you know.

You're not Scots?

*

UNION

'That this House believes in this House'

. . . and several maidens are to be congratulated on their first appearance at the dispatch box: D. Hope (Trinity), S. Whitehorn (BNC) and J. Dunn (Hall) sporting a most impressive pair of black eyes.

Isis

*

Hello, you're Israel Dunn aren't you?

Oh, yes, Jack. It's Alex. Alex Silverleaf? From school.

I heard you'd come up. My mother ran into your aunt the other day, Mrs Fondler. This is my second year. Are you settling in all right? I was rather surprised when I heard you were here. There are not many, er, I mean, well you know, the Hall's one of the more traditional colleges, isn't it?

Well feel free to look me up any time. I'm at Trinity. Do you know about the J. Soc.?

The Jewish Society. I'm secretary this year. You should come along to one of our Friday night meals at Long John's.

Do you know Long John's? The kosher restaurant, Mr Silver is a leading member of the Oxford congregation.

*

CHERWELL POETRY COMPETITION

First Prize of 3 guineas to Peter Middlebrooke for 'Notes on the Psychology of Poetry'.

Second Prize of 1 guinea to Richard Fouldes for 'Night with a Greek Girl'.

Third Prize of ½ guinea to J. Dunn for 'Laburnums'.

Cherwell

*

Jack, please, don't.

I do like you, Jack, I like you very much, but you know, I can't, I'm Catholic.

*

Berlin were you? Lucky bugger. I was in bloody Palestine, it was hell. Imshi, that means get lost in Arabic, it was the only word I learned. Only one you needed, that and a boot up the rearside. It's the best thing we ever did getting out of there. Let the Yids and Arabs kill each other, that's what I always said.

*

'PERICLES'

... and Jack Dunn as variously a fisherman, a messenger and a gentleman.

Cherwell

*

My God, chaps, you should go and have a look at what I've just seen in the porters' lodge.

You tell me. But whatever they are there's a whole blinking tribe of them. All wearing the oddest clothes and talking some language I've never heard before. One of them was carrying some bag with a foreign name on it and the most horrible smell coming out of it. The peculiar thing was the female of the species are all identical, or at least the two of them in the porters' lodge were. Thought I was seeing double, decided I must have had too much mother's ruin last night.

Are you all right Dunn? You don't look so well.

Good idea, I think I'll have a lie down myself.

*

Dunn, are you in there? Dunn? Dunn? I know it's late but it's an emergency. Whisson here's got some cookie in his room and he needs one of your whatnots. Blast, I don't think he's in. He's bound to be back soon. He's got a box of them, army issue, he's been keeping the whole college supplied. Doesn't even charge for them which is something for a Jew.

Do you think you can keep her going until he gets back? Oh, Dunn, you are in there. Good show.

*

Hello Israel.

Sorry, Jack, I must remember. Did you have a nice time with your family? I heard they'd been down last Sunday. Did they take you anywhere good for lunch?

Oh, that's nice. I haven't seen you at the J. Soc.

I know there's always so much to do. I tell you what I'll drop round a list of events for the term, then maybe you can have a chance to plan ahead.

*

What I don't understand old fellow is why you didn't just read English. I'm studying the blasted subject and you read more poetry and novels than I do.

Oh you don't want to be worrying about that now. Now is the time to acquire knowledge and expand your mind. I've got no idea what I'm going to do when I leave and frankly I haven't spent a minute thinking about it.

*

Come on, Jack, you've really got to go now. It's very late and I need to go to bed.

Jack, please.

*

This is hilarious, Jack. Listen to this. The Very Rev. the Hamam on 'Folk Law of the Sephardim in the Maghreb'. Do people really go to these talks? And on a Saturday night? Haven't they got anything better to do? What about this one. 'The Future of the Torah in Israel'. Can't they get anyone to speak on something more interesting than that. And look at their names. Can there really be somebody called Rabbi Hayyim Frumstein. What kind of name is that? I think they're made up. It's a fraud. Really they're probably having boozy parties and eating bacon sandwiches.

What?

You wouldn't.

*

Where are you going with all those books, Dunn? Not working again are you? You'll give us all a bad name. Why don't you stop being such a trog and come and have tea.

*

CRICKET CUPPERS

Christchurch beat Hall easily in the first round of Cuppers, scoring 160 and bowling out Hall for 38. Among the runs for Christchurch was C. R. S. Winstanley with 78 while D. Bardolph took six wickets for 12 runs. For Hall J. Dunn carried his bat for 6 not out.

Isis

*

Look, Jack, we broke up a month ago, so I really don't think it's any business of yours whether I spent the night with Michael or not, but if you really want to know I did.

That's the whole point, Jack darling. I'm a Catholic and so is Michael, don't you see?

*

Why have you always got to be so stiff-necked, Dunn?

*

'THE COLD SEA'

. . . and Jack Dunn as a bearded sailor.

*

I don't know why you never go for girls of your own sort, Jack. If you ask me they're damned exotic.

*

WANDERING JEW

Those of us foolish enough to be painting the town red last Saturday night missed the surprise event of the evening in the gathering of the OU Jewish Society, where the guest speaker was a certain Mr. Zvi Hanegbi, currently of Marseilles, latterly of the Haganah, and author of several venerable tomes.

Arriving late, in a dark suit, thick glasses and a heavy beard, and puffing away at a large cheroot, Mr. Hanegbi enlivened the evening with his tales of hashish smuggling, Middle Eastern immorality, the shooting of deserters and finally his own desertion from the Israeli army.

So heated was the subject matter that after a time the Senior Member, Mr. Friedman, was seen to remove his spectacles and polish the steam from them before putting them back on his nose and peering closely at the speaker. 'A most interesting if unusual evening,' was Mr. Friedman's comment when the speech concluded.

Soon after, having pleaded another appointment, Mr. Hanegbi left and a little later a person matching his description, save that he had no beard, was spotted buying a round of drinks in the Hall bar.

Isis

*

Are you sure you're not musical darling? I've always wanted to do it with one of you, I hear you are so sensual.

*

You've never sailed? Well you simply must. Where have you been all your life? Come down to the lake any Saturday and I'll take you out. It's not like the sea, I'm afraid, but if the wind picks up you can have a pleasant little potter.

*

She's too thin for my liking. I prefer a little flesh, I've never gone for the Belsen type.

*

It'll be fun, Jack, there's half a dozen of us going, we pop over to Paris for the weekend, find somewhere to stay, have a few drinks, some French food.

Are you sure?

That Ann Wenham you like is going.

*

Dear Mr. Dunn,

I am writing to let you know that your account is overdrawn by the amount of £234. 13s. 4d. Perhaps at your convenience you will see to remedying this situation.

Yours sincerely,

William Archer

Assistant Manager

*

Jack, you know Julia.

You don't? How strange. Well now you do. Jack Dunn meet Julia Rosenthal.

*

You do understand the difficulties for a man without a private income at the Bar, Mr. Dunn. I have known barristers wait ten years for their first brief and if that is a little unusual it generally does take some time to build up a practice on which one can live. Unless of course you have contacts that can give you a head start, but in your case, well, you are going to need some other source of income. I can't persuade you at least to speak to one or two firms of solicitors? It really might be the more sensible option. You would be earning right away and I have no doubt we can find the right firm for you. Nowhere dusty, a good sharp firm, with partners who would be sure to like the cut of your jib, if you pardon the expression.

*

God, those examiners wanted their pound of flesh.

*

Look who it is, it's my old friend Dunn. What are you drinking? Barman another one of whatever my friend here is drinking. No, no, no, I won't take no for an answer,

Dunn. I want to buy you a drink. You see I like you Dunn. I think you're a good fellow. I don't want you to listen to what those others say Dunn. You're a good fellow. Let them say what they want. What do they know? A good fellow that's what you are Dunn. A good fellow despite everything. A jolly, jolly, jolly, jolly good fellow.

Lamentations

London, 1954

Take off your coat, Jack. Let me hang it up for you. What would you like to drink? Some tea? Coffee? I have some cake if you would like a little slice.

Julia's not back yet. She telephoned to say she would be a little late. They are having a meeting at the school, all the teachers. Sit down, she won't be long. It's nice for me to get a chance to talk to you. Julia doesn't tell me anything about you. She thinks I'm interfering that I want to know a little about my only daughter's boyfriend. When I was young I always thought I would have a big family. I wanted to have five children at least. Then that horrible man came to power and it became a crime to bring an innocent child into the world. I wouldn't have had Julia if I had known what was going to happen while I was carrying her. But how could I know? Nobody knew. It was unimaginable.

Listen to me. I promised not to bore you and that is what I am doing. You don't want to sit here listening to an old woman going on. You are probably thinking why doesn't that horrible old monster shut up. You can't imagine that I was once a pretty young girl like Julia, can you? Well don't take my word for it. Ask Heinrich when he comes home. When I was a girl I had dozens of men chasing me. I was a real beauty. When they voted in school for the girl to be Germania you know who they chose? Of course that was before all this horribleness that made me lose my looks. I'm forty-seven years old, I look sixty.

Ach, Jack, if you could have seen me then. My eyes weren't tired and grey, they were blue, bright blue and my hair was pale brown, almost blond. I was the most admired girl in the school. With my cornflower blue eyes and lovely singing voice and straight back you wouldn't have known I was Jewish. Stand straight my father always told me. Stand straight and don't move your hands about when you are talking.

Such a marvellous man he was. So handsome and always perfectly turned out. Every weekend he took us for a treat. In the summer to the lake for a picnic or walking through the woods to a picturesque inn to drink Himbeersaft while he had his beer. In the winter, skating on the rink they made out of the tennis court. He was the best skater in Berlin. Backwards, forwards, one foot in the air, one eye closed. To be a German living in Berlin was to be the luckiest person in the world he always said. There was no crime. The children could play safely in the street. Young people could make love without a worry on the benches on Unter Den Linden.

I can still remember the shock of looking out of the window from the train coming into London. I had never seen anything like those rows and rows of identical dirty grey houses. I was used to Tiergarten with its elegant apartment buildings with wrought-iron balconies and manicured gardens and central heating and lifts. In Berlin nobody climbed stairs, since I came here I have spent my whole life climbing up and down. We had a fireplace in my father's study, we called it the English fire, he would light it in the evenings and we would sit and admire the dancing flames. Never in my life did I dream I would one day have to rely on such a fire to keep my family warm through a freezing damp English winter, the wind whistling through the gaps in the windows. In Berlin the windows are made properly, with nice wide sills to put plants on. Look at my poor plants here, I have to put the pots on the floor, it's impossible to keep them alive.

Enough, enough. I want to hear about you Jack. I don't want you to think I'm some ungrateful old woman complaining about England. This is my country now, I am English, I have an English passport. Only it was not easy for us coming from our beautiful flat in Berlin to that shabby little room in Swiss Cottage with a shared gas ring and a toilet between ten people. Our first night there, Julia would not stop crying and asking when we were going to go home. For me it didn't matter, I didn't care about myself, but for Julia, and poor Heinrich, he could not understand what had happened to him. In all of Berlin there was no one who knew the German language better than Heinrich. For seven years he had been compiling the new German dictionary. It was like the Oxford Dictionary here, every German would have had to have a copy in their house. When they took his job away from him at the university the publishers told him, Don't worry, we will pay your salary, please keep writing your dictionary, it will be the standard work for a hundred years. Then suddenly we were here in London where nobody was interested in a professor of German philology. You know for yourself he is not a worldly man. When he was awarded his doctorate the thesis was so brilliant the university held a soirée in his honour, he walked into the room and all these professors standing there started sniffing at this strange smell, they couldn't understand what it was. It was the fish his landlady had sent him out to buy the day before, he had put it in his pocket and forgotten all about it.

You wouldn't believe it, but when I was young we had servants to do everything for us. On Sunday on their day off we thought it was a treat to heat up some food that had been left and wash up the plates. In England the only work

I could get was as a maid scrubbing floors and emptying chamber-pots. I had to learn how to polish silver and fold napkins and behave like a little mouse, seen and not heard. Every day I took my apron and cap in a bag and changed in a public convenience so Heinrich and Julia would not see me in my uniform. Then I got on the bus and tried to improve my English by listening to the people speaking. By God, what kind of English. At school I studied English for six years, I was the best English speaker in the class, the teacher said I had a perfect accent, but sitting on that bus I could not understand a word they spoke. For years I was convinced the conductor was shouting old tie, like the expression, old school tie.

Heinrich said if I could be a maid he could be a butler, but he did not even know how to boil an egg. In the morning he would take Julia to school and sit in a café drinking one cup of coffee all day. I couldn't afford to buy a pair of silk stockings, I had to buy one stocking at a time so I never had two that properly matched. Eventually Heinrich got a job lifting books in a warehouse. In Berlin every night people who wrote books came to our house, brilliant people, artists, intellectuals, philosophers, even a Sikh with a turban, and now he was lifting books for a few shillings a week.

Even that was better than when the war came. A bomb fell on his warehouse and he lost his job. We were lucky they didn't intern us, though we had to report to the police every week as enemy aliens. We weren't allowed maps or German books or even a radio to listen to the news. It was only because the walls were so thin that I could put my ear to the wallpaper and find out who was winning the war from the neighbour's radio. When I went out to buy food, people would hear my voice and call me a bloody German and tell me to get out. Our own daughter was ashamed of us. She wouldn't let me talk in front of her friends, she never brought a friend home, she always had to go to their house. She hated everything about Germany. When I talked about Berlin she would put her hands over her ears and sing 'God Save the Queen'. I brought from Berlin this set of little dolls. We had to bring only the essentials but I could not leave those dolls. That was why my parents stayed. When I begged them to leave with us they said how could they go without their things. Their things and their friends and the life they were used to. They were tiny those dolls. I wrapped them in paper and hid them inside Heinrich's socks. They belonged with this beautiful dolls' house that had been mine when I was a child. It had the most perfect furniture and carpets and wallpaper on the walls. Julia loved it more than anything in the world, but as soon as she went to school in England she refused to play with the dolls. I had to put them away. I still have them somewhere.

She wouldn't speak German, she wouldn't listen to me if I did. For years she barely communicated with her father.

When he tried to persuade her to read Heine and Schiller, to see what a wonderful culture there had been in Germany, she shouted at him. Shouting at her father, this great professor, it broke his heart. She would only read English books. The only music she would listen to was this American Jazz you young people like. I was brought up to appreciate great literature and Classical music. Every week we went to the Galerie Friedlander to hear lectures on modern art and plays at the Deutsche Teatre. The best German playwrights like Goethe and Lessing and the foreigners translated into German by translators more brilliant even than the original writers. Last year I persuaded Heinrich to come with me to see 'King Lear' in the West End. It was such a disappointment, so drab. Shakespeare is so much more noble in German.

Nuptials

London, 1956

Waiter, over here, excuse me but I think there's been some mistake, we've been put on the wrong table.

Don't tell me to calm down, Pessie, I'm talking to this nice young man.

I'm sorry, as I was saying, I think there's been a mistake. The bridegroom's mother Mrs Golda Dunn is my first cousin, I am sure she would not have put us on a table by the toilet where we can't even see the bride and groom.

She did? Herself?

I've never been so insulted in my life.

*

Don't get up, Eli, I just came over to say mazel tov and to put a little something in your pocket for the bride and bridegroom. They make a lovely couple.

So tell me has Israel gone to the Bar yet?

What's the matter? He's an Oxford boy, he can't work for Victor Fondler all his life. I thought it was just for a year until he'd saved a little money. An Oxford boy shouldn't be working in ladieswear, it's a waste of a good mind. At least if he's not going to the Bar let him come and talk to me, I've got something big going with these partitions.

*

That's the bride's mother, Mrs Rosenthal, and her husband in the Berlin worsted, the Doctor Professor.

Well don't be. You know the joke. You stand in Swiss Cottage and shout Herr Doctor Professor twenty heads turn. It's true. Bernard tried it once from the bus, he counted seven men looked round. You want me to introduce you?

*

Israel, what's the big hurry? Stop and talk to me for a minute. That's a beautiful bride let me tell you. If I was thirty years younger I'd knock you out and take her myself.

You think I couldn't still do it. Come on then, put your hands up. A left, a right. Oh my God. Israel, are you all right? What's happened to your nose, is it bleeding. Hold your head back, don't let it drip on your shirt. Here take my handkerchief. Keep your head back.

Nothing's going on, don't worry the boy, he's just got a little nose bleed that's all.

I didn't do anything to him. My hand slipped.

I know it's his wedding day, you think I don't know it's his wedding day. What am I, an idiot?

*

That's Eli's mother from South Africa and her sister Bella. She lives here now. She came over two or three years ago.

Not Bella, she's from Leeds. The mother, Pearl. Her husband was the one who took her to live in the jungle and lost all the family money. That's her daughter Rosa over there, Eli's sister, and her husband the skinny one. Don't they make a pretty pair? She must eat all the food she cooks before it reaches his plate.

*

What? Do you think he's going to work in shmutter all his life? He's an Oxford boy. Golda explained everything to me. To get on at the Bar, you need to be married. Next week he's leaving Vizelda. Within ten years he'll be a judge.

*

A flatlet in Chelsea? What do they want with Chelsea? Why can't they live in Golders Green like everyone else?

*

Julia, kumen, mazel tov, mazel tov. I grandmuzzer now, I tell you must eat. Eat, eat. Men don't like thin girl.

*

With the staring eyes? That's Neville, the intense one, Ruthie's boyfriend. He's a committed Zionist. He refused to go to university, he's at some farm in Sussex training to go and live on a kibbutz. Eli and Golda are keeping their fingers crossed that when Ruthie goes up to university she'll drop him and find someone more suitable.

*

He's no fool. He's an Oxford boy. He can see an opportunity when it's in front of him. Vizelda's a nice business and Victor's not so young any more. Who's going to take over when he dies? None of the shlemiels his daughters have married, that's for sure. It's simply a matter of whether Israel can show the magic touch with ladies fashion.

*

A German he has to marry. He always was a rebel ever since he was a little boy.

*

See the two old ladies with the white hair? I think one of them must be the hottentot.

223

You know the hottentot, Jack's grandmother. The one he told us about. She claims to be Jewish but Jack thinks his father found her in Africa. The only language she's supposed to be able to speak is Yiddish but when Jack bought her a Yiddish newspaper she tried to read it upside down.

*

The way I heard it Eli and Golda were just happy she was a girl. All the time he was at Oxford they never met a single girlfriend. They were beginning to worry he was that way.

That way. A feigeleh.

I didn't say he was a feigeleh, I said they were worried he was a feigeleh. For God's sake keep your voice down, it's the boy's wedding day.

*

Sailing in the South of France? What do they want with the South of France? Why can't they go on honeymoon to Bournemouth like everyone else?

Ruth

Galilee, 1957–8

23 Adar. Walking down to the dairy this morning to fetch the milk for breakfast I watched the sunlight move across the lake as if the water were waking from some ancient sleep. That is what it feels like here. The Jewish people and the Jewish land are awakening again after 2 thousand years. A few years ago there was nothing but dry grass and dust and now this brave little settlement with its simple white buildings and orchards laid out in perfect rows and green irrigated fields has grown up out of the hillside. How silly all the fuss we left behind in London seems now. Nobody here asks where we were married or whether I finished my degree. What matters is whether you can plough the land or milk the cows. If my family would only come here and see what it is like they would understand. Being here wakes up the Jewishness inside each of us. I am

225

sure if Jack was here he would see that Naphtali's insistence on calling him Israel is quite different from his calling Naphtali Neville. I almost wish I didn't have a Jewish name so I could change mine too, though I like it that Ruth is pronounced 'Root' here, it makes me feel that I am putting down roots.

25 Adar. A week since we arrived. Last night we looked on the notice board and were excited to see we were both on dining-room duty. When the night-watchman banged on our door at 5.15 we leaped out of bed together and walked holding hands through the darkness to work. Naphtali did get told off for washing the floor the wrong way. He asked Noa why it mattered, but she flashed her black eyes at him and told him that's the way they always do it, and he accepted it in a way he never would have at home. It's because he is where he wants to be here, doing what he wants to be doing, though he can't wait to get out into the fields. It is hard work laying the tables, serving the food, clearing up and then just when breakfast is all put away having to get everything ready for lunch. But what would have seemed boring is full of meaning here. Like the food. At first I was rather surprised at the food, it is like going back to rationing, I thought being on a farm we would have more fresh meat and fruit and vegetables. But as Naphtali says food is fuel, and giving it any

other significance is bourgeois. It's the same with so many things. Shirley and Pamela would shriek if they saw me dressed so plainly without even a dash of lipstick in the evening but lipstick here would seem ridiculous. I am happier in my work clothes and one good dress from the store than I would be in the smartest frock at home. I love our plain bare little room. I love the simple pleasures, a shower at the end of the day, going to the dining-hall and sitting in the first free seat, joining in whatever evening activities are arranged. When we get into bed we fall asleep within seconds. It is a simple honest life, without hypocrisy or pretension.

29 Adar. Our first letter from home, from Mummy with a little note at the end from Daddy. So they have survived my leaving after all! In fact they seem unaffected in any way. Most of the letter is taken up with Mummy going on about some row between Xenia Green and Betty Noyk, as if I could possibly be interested. Uncle Victor has finally bought Jack the car he has been promising. It is a Sunbeam. I am quite content with the sunbeams we have here, beaming from an azure sky.

1 Nissan. Ilana said we should not be corks for much longer. That is the word for people bobbing from one job to another. I was in the toddler's house today and Naphtali

was on sanitation duty. I felt a bit sorry for him but he said all tasks here are sacred ones. It was exhausting in the toddler's house but very rewarding and fascinating. The children even at such a young age seem so different to English children. Living communally they are not spoiled or clingy. They have to share everything, toys, living space, food, grown-ups. It seems to work wonderfully for everyone. For the children the kibbutz is like an enormous family with dozens of brothers and sisters and aunts and uncles, while the mothers are emancipated from domesticity and can go out to work. Mummy is so scathing about this life but that is exactly what she always complains she was never able to do with her creations. Then the two hours that parents get with their children they really enjoy and make the most of, whereas I can't ever remember Mummy or Daddy playing with me for two whole hours.

3 Nissan. Naphtali took his pillow back to the stores this afternoon. Gershon, who he has been working with in sanitation, recently came back from the army and sleeps on the floor with only a blanket wrapped around him. I don't mind the pillow, but I am putting my foot down about the floor. We have barely been married a month!

5 Nissan. We went to the film-show last night. The screen is a sheet and the projector very old and flickery but it all

added to the atmosphere. It was a Czech film with Hebrew subtitles, so I found it hard to follow, but its portrayal of peasant life felt very real compared to the kind of films we used to go to see at home, though I didn't mind when Naphtali suggested we leave half way as it was very long and I was very tired. His neck was sore, he cricked it at work. He is going to get back his pillow until his neck is better.

6 Nissan. Yesterday was one of the happiest days of our lives. The oranges had all ripened at once in the orchard and had to be got down before they fell and were ruined, so an emergency meeting was called and it was agreed that the whole kibbutz should spend the Sabbath picking oranges. Everyone was there, even the children. Some climbed the ladders, others picked what could be reached from the ground, others put the fruit in sacks. We even got to have lots of oranges, normally the fruit goes straight off for sale, but there were so many bruised and overripe ones that we ate until our faces and hands and clothes were dripping with sweet sticky juice. At lunch-time the kitchen staff brought out bread and salad and after we had eaten we worked again singing and laughing and talking until nightfall. We really felt like pioneers and all day today I have felt as if I really belong, as if yesterday were some kind of initiation.

9 Nissan. We have been assigned our permanent jobs! Naphtali's is in the orchards and I am in the laundry. I was rather hoping to be outside too, maybe the gardens, but it will only be for a year or two and we have our whole lives here ahead of us and laundry is as important as anything else in the running of the kibbutz.

14 Nissan. I have been too tired to write anything the last few days. The laundry really is hard labour which is not surprising seeing how dirty Naphtali is when he comes home from work. He seems to spend his whole day making clothes dirty while I spend mine cleaning them again. I only hope I will toughen up like the other women. Ganit, who I work with, is one of the original members of the kibbutz, and she seems tireless. She has been telling me about the early days. It sounds like every day was like the orange day. Men and women working side by side to clear the land, digging for water, planting the first trees and crops, sleeping in tents and every evening singing songs around the fires and dancing the horra until they fell asleep exhausted. I said it must be rather dull for her in the laundry now but she said someone must do it, though of the nine people working in the laundry eight of us are women and only one man.

17 Nissan. Naphtali is getting a bit frustrated in the orchards because the old hands don't have time to explain

things properly or teach him. He knows they are very stretched but he says if he knew more he could be more useful, as it is he often stands around doing nothing. The truth is the Kibbutz is short of people. It particularly affects agriculture, as however much you plan there are always going to be busier times in the fields and orchards. I told Naphtali he must be patient and wait for a slower time then it will get better.

23 Nissan. Our first Seder in Israel. It was so moving to be celebrating the festival of freedom in our own land. Everyone stopped work early to have showers and dress in our best clothes and go to the dining hall, which looked beautiful. The older children had been painting the walls for days with harvest scenes and pictures from Exodus and the younger ones collected flowers to put on the white cloths which lay on every table. The readings were not only from the Haggadah, but from modern books, and poems and things people here have written about freedom and the meaning of spring and renewal. In between we sung old and new songs and the children did a lovely little performance of Israeli folk dances. Passover has always been my favourite festival, but here it really has meaning. The kitchen had gone out of the way to make a wonderful meal too, not entirely traditional, but we stuffed ourselves on chicken and fish and fresh fruit and vegetables. Then we danced the

horra for what seemed like hours and hours, round and round, though I eventually had to stop, I felt exhausted, but Naphtali was like a dervish, stamping his feet, jumping, his eyes sparkling.

5 Iyar. I am pregnant! I suppose I have known for about a week but at first I couldn't take it in and then I wanted to be sure before I wrote those words. When I missed I thought it was probably moving here and everything but then I started feeling sick. Ganit was once a midwife and she examined me and said I am definitely pregnant. She was so matter of fact about it I had to pretend to be too and carry on working when all I wanted was to run and find Naphtali. In the end I couldn't stand it, and said I was feeling sick, and ran all the way down to the orchards. Then I really did feel sick and threw up against one of the orange trees before I managed to get the words out. The baby will be Israeli. A sabra!

27 Iyar. It is Shabbat and with both of us off we had planned a lovely lazy day together. It is getting very hot and I am tired all the time and I had been looking forward to lying in with Naphtali until 10, but at 6 a.m. there was a knock at the door and it was Michael saying there had been a leak in the irrigation system or something and volunteers were needed. Naphtali went of course. I had my lie-in but it

wasn't the same, though at least at breakfast there was halva and cake, which I got stuck into. I crave sweet things all the time and it doesn't matter how much saccharine water you put in tea, it just doesn't satisfy. I do think they should really make allowances for pregnant women. Can it be good for the baby to get so little meat?

7 Sivan. We were sitting having breakfast this morning when Boaz came round asking if anyone wanted to go down to the lake for a swim. We jumped at the chance and had a magical morning. Twenty of us rode down in the back of the lorry. It is the first time since we arrived that we have been out of the kibbutz and it was very strange to go from our modern socialistic kibbutz into this almost Biblical landscape of tiny villages with scrawny chickens scratching in the dust and old Arab men with weather-beaten faces sitting in the shade as they have done for hundreds of years. We are the future and they are the past. I wonder if that is how they see it. The lake was beautiful and the water was deliciously cold. We swam and splashed and lay on the banks and I felt cool during the day for the first time in weeks, though half way back up the hill again we were as hot and sweaty as if we had never been in the water. Boaz said there is talk of building a swimming pool in the kibbutz, as it is only seldom that people can get down to the lake. It would be very nice, but I am sure it won't happen. It somehow seems

so against the grain of what the kibbutz is all about. Too decadent.

13 Tammuz. Naphtali started his two weeks of guard duty last night. I found it hard to sleep without him, and worrying about him. He was very proud to be carrying a real loaded gun but I was quite relieved this morning to find that he had not shot himself in the foot or something.

17 Tammuz. We had an English film last night, Passport to Pimlico with Margaret Rutherford and Stanley Holloway. We English found it hilarious and were rolling about in the aisles while all the others were completely bemused by the humour and kept staring at us almost crossly. I haven't laughed so much since we got here and I began to worry about the baby. Can you lose a baby by laughing?

24 Tammuz. Naphtali was very upset when I saw him at lunch-time. Half an hour after he started work this morning the lorry arrived with twenty men from the immigrant village on the other side of the valley. They had been hired to help with the apple and plum harvest. Nothing had been said at any of the meetings and it was a surprise to many of the orchard workers. Dan said a decision had had to be made quickly or we would have lost a lot of the fruit, which we can't afford as these harvests are big cash earners. They

are bigger orchards than the orange ones and even if the whole kibbutz helped it would take a week of evenings and the whole Sabbath to pick the harvest and people have to have time off and to see their children. It does seem against the principles of self-sufficiency and collectivism which are the basis of the kibbutz. If every time we have a problem we go and hire people to sort it out for us how are we different from any other society? But it is an emergency and only for one week and the immigrants are Jews and apparently need work badly. Shortly before we came Ben Gurion made an appeal to the kibbutzes to give employment to them when they could. I do not quite understand it, but they don't seem to have found their place in Israel yet. They are mostly from Rumania and Yemen and places like that, they came after the war, and they are still living in temporary villages.

23 Elul. It was a really heated meeting last night, this time about the swimming pool. We are beginning to see that there is a divide in the kibbutz. On the one side are the newer members like us. We are mostly younger and English and idealistic – it was ideals after all that brought us here. On the other are the old hands who have been here since the early days. These differences were there in the discussion about the immigrant workers and were apparent again last night. Uri made a speech about the years spent clearing the land with their bare hands, when they had no money for anything,

when the future of the kibbutz was in doubt, and how now they have earned the right to have a few simple luxuries. I found it quite moving and couldn't help thinking he was right, but then David who works with Naphtali in the orchard asked where the money was coming from for the swimming pool – from the sale of the plums and apples picked by the hired immigrant labour? The arguing went on for two hours and Naphtali stood up at one point and said that if people didn't like the heat why had they come here in the first place. In the end it was decided to have a vote at a later date.

2 Tishri. Our first New Year in Israel. We had a big feast with lots of lovely food and wine. It was really reaffirming after the recent arguments, which were made to seem very silly by the skits people put on. One that Roni did was about the swimming pool. He played everyone, the Hebrew speakers splashing and laughing in an imaginary pool, and the English speakers standing with their backs to the water saying it wasn't really that hot while wiping the sweat from their brows. I was worried Naphtali might not find it funny but even he was smiling. Festivals here are so much more honest than at home where people who do nothing all year buy up their seats in the shul for the High Holy Days.

18 Tishri. A letter from Mummy. Julia is pregnant too! I so hope the cousins will have a chance to be friends. Apparently

Julia is suffering a lot from sickness, I am sure it is the climate as I had only a few bad days. She is going to give up her teaching job at the end of the term. Victor has made Jack Managing Director of Vizelda, with him as Chairman. Mummy thinks maybe Victor will retire at seventy and let Jack take over. It still seems odd to think of Jack at Vizelda, I wonder if he really likes doing it. The sad news is that Uncle Boris has died in South Africa. I think since Grandma Pearl died he must have been the last of that generation.

2 Cheshvan. Naphtali has been moved to the chicken house. With the rain, and the time of year, there is not much work in the orchard, and he has been temporarily reassigned. It is frustrating for him, as he had hoped this might be the time when he could learn more about orchardry, or whatever the word is. Some have stayed on in the orchards but Naphtali has not been very popular with Dan these last months. He came home today covered in dust from chicken-feed and looking rather sorry for himself.

9 Cheshvan. It is very cold. Thank God for the oil stove. This luxury Naphtali can't complain about, as it stops his now very pregnant wife from freezing to death.

29 Kislev. Our baby daughter was born three days ago on the second day of Hanukah. We have called her Yael. A

Hanukah baby is good luck everyone says. I am more exhausted than I could have imagined, but she is very beautiful and wonderful. She looks just like Naphtali, the same dark brow and fierce eyes.

8 Tebet. I am so tired. Every night I have to get up three or four times to go and feed Yael in the baby house, trudging through the dark and mud to get there. By the time I have fed her, calmed her down, put her back into her cot, got back here, dried myself, climbed into bed and settled down, it seems the next knock comes at the door. She is not allowed even to visit our room for six months. I am not sure if I am going to survive that long.

17 Tebet. Naphtali is back in the orchards, thank God, as he was beginning to go mad bobbing here and there. He sneaked home three deliciously sweet oranges this evening, which I ate all at once. I was surprised, but he has always thought the kibbutz should devote less of its resources to cash crops and more to growing food for us to eat.

11 Shebat. My first day back at work. I wanted to cry the whole time. It was only four hours but I am so tired and all I thought about was little Yael in the baby house. I am sure it is because I am tired but it all seems upside down. I know I am supposed to be emancipated from domesticity but I

don't feel very emancipated washing other people's clothes in the laundry while someone else looks after Yael.

15 Shebat. Tu Bishevat. A happy day, reminding us why we are here. The whole kibbutz, even Yael in my arms, went around the gardens digging holes and planting saplings. The children danced and everyone sang. Naphtali dug our hole and held Yael while he let me plant our tree as he is going to be planting hundreds in the next few weeks.

19 Shebat. Naphtali is very miserable and is even talking about leaving the kibbutz. He said he has dreamed all his life about planting trees in the soil of Israel, that for him it should have been as close to a religious experience as he could ever have, but the whole thing has been sullied for him by the hiring of the immigrant workers again. He says it is straightforward capitalism, the orchards are being run like a business, we are the employer and the immigrants are the exploited labour. They do the donkey-work, digging the holes, while the kibbutzniks go behind them planting the saplings. I think he is overreacting a bit but it does seem odd that the kibbutz already has more orchards than it can look after itself yet is bringing in outside workers to plant more trees. The truth is I don't know what to think. I am so tired that I find it hard to cope with anything like this. Maybe we should leave. If we went back to England at least I could

keep Yael with me at night and be with her all day if I wanted. I know it would be like a defeat, and I don't want that, but what is the point of staying here if all three of us are miserable?

28 Shebat. Naphtali had a big row with Dan in the orchards in front of everybody, including the immigrant workers. He had been talking to the immigrants about their village, most of them still live in corrugated iron shacks, with no running water and no jobs. He finally asked Dan if it was really necessary to employ the immigrant workers then why didn't they give them a proper wage rather than piece-work, i.e., a certain sum for every hole they dig. Dan said that had been tried at first, but the immigrants had just sat around all day, they needed an incentive to work. So Naphtali said, what about giving them shares in the profit, bringing them partly into the collective. Well apparently everyone was now gathered around, kibbutzim and immigrants. Someone said the immigrants could join the kibbutz if they wanted but instead they chose to sit around in the immigrant village living off government handouts. Someone else asked if the immigrants had shared in the losses the kibbutz made in its early years. Anyway the upshot was the immigrants didn't like being talked about like that and put down spades and refused to work and Dan blamed Naphtali but Naphtali is unrepentant. He says it is pure and simple exploitation and he didn't

come here to exploit his fellow Jews. He thinks maybe we came to the wrong place, we should have gone to help build one of the new towns they are making out of the desert, at least the new towns are unwritten books, whoever builds them can influence how they turn out. I don't know, I am not sure if I could cope with starting all over again.

3 Adar. The hamsin has come. It is horrible, hot dust blowing everywhere. Poor little Yael is miserable, all she wants to do is snuggle up on my breast and feed. The minute I take her off she starts snuffling and coughing and crying. I have been staying virtually the whole night in the baby house and next week I am due to be up to six hours at the laundry. I don't know how I am going to manage it. The wind has killed all the flowers and covered everything in brown dust. The swimming pool vote is tonight, I must say I am tempted to vote for it.

28 Elul. We have been here a week but this is the first chance I have had to write anything. It can hardly be called a new town yet, just a few dozen asbestos huts like this one, but I don't mind. I am happy simply to be here. Our hut is comfortable, with two rooms, our own kitchen and shower and a little verandah. Last night for the first time in her life Yael slept happily through the night in her cot beside our bed. Naphtali has gone off to work with the sandwiches I made

him in his pocket. He is clearing ground for the new houses and very happy about it. He works in a team with six Bedouin, the foreman is also a Bedouin. He works with a turia like a real pioneer. Yesterday he came home very proud of himself as the Bedouin have been teaching him how to swear in Arabic. He can say you are the armpit of your mother's goat or something. We even had our first letter here yesterday, from Julia enclosing some lovely pictures of Helen. She and Jack are looking for a little house to buy, preferably nearer the grandparents than Chelsea. She sent a clipping from the Clothing Manufacturer's Gazette showing Jack and Uncle Victor standing next to each other arm in arm like father and son. I wonder what Daddy must think.

2 Chronicles

From The Businessman, *1963*

MAN OF THE MOMENT

No company in Britain is more demanding than Marks & Spencer so it was by no means an ordinary day's business last month when the top retailer awarded a million-pound contract to a little-known supplier headed by a 33-year-old in only his fourth year of running his own company. But then Jack Dunn, MD and main shareholder in Tennyson Textiles, is no ordinary clothing manufacturer.

For one thing he is Oxford-educated and a qualified barrister. For another, after a decade of success, and despite his growing reputation, he still thinks of himself as only temporarily in the business. 'If you told me when I was at Oxford that this is what I would be doing in ten years time I would have laughed,' he said. His time there was spent rowing, acting and speaking at the Union, activities at which one doesn't doubt he was successful, though he dismisses further questions with a modest wave of the hand. 'I never meant to be a businessman and I still don't really think of myself as one, which is perhaps an advantage. I've never been afraid of taking a risk that might end in bankruptcy.'

His intention at Oxford was to go the Bar but when he got there he found it too restrictive. 'I didn't like having to dress formally and conform to other people's idea of what I should be.' Not knowing what to do he turned to a distant relative who owned a small company making women's clothes for the lower end of the market, where he had worked in his vacations from Oxford driving a delivery van and calling customers to pay off his overdraft. 'It was pure serendipity,' Dunn says. 'I needed some temporary work and had not the slightest intention of staying; I was only taken on as a favour to the family. In order to make sure I didn't do too much damage in any one part of the business, I kept being moved from one job to another. By the end of six months I had accidentally completed a sort of quick-fire graduate trainee programme. I had a pretty good idea of how the business worked and one or two ideas how to improve it.'

Dunn took his ideas to his relative, and before he knew it they had started to make money for the company. Within two years profits had increased by 40 per cent on the same turnover, and with the company able to pass on the benefits of its reduced costs to its customers, volume quickly began to rise as well. 'To my surprise I was having fun,' Dunn says. 'It was a challenge to come up with ideas and see if they worked.' He stayed for six years until he reached a watershed: he had to decide whether to continue working for someone else or strike out on his own. With an amicable farewell to his relative he took the latter course.

In an industry thick with chaff, it was not hard to find ailing concerns ripe for takeover. The problem was to raise the capital. By another stroke of serendipity, at this moment he was left a legacy of £10,000 by an uncle in South Africa, and with that as his contribution he went cap in hand round the City to raise the rest. It is a testament to both his capabilities and the foresight of the banks that he was able to raise the cash he was seeking and remain the primary shareholder in the business.

The company he purchased, Bradleigh, was a third-generation family concern. It consisted of three factories, in London, Slough and Nottingham, and in 1959 had suffered a net loss of £32,000. Dunn renamed it Tennyson, after his favourite poet, and applied the medicine he had practised in his relative's factory. He cut staff, improved working conditions, introduced new systems for costings and quality control, spent money on plant, especially automated plant, and sold himself hard to customers. His first break came after two years with a contract with Woolworth, and now he has cracked the big one, Marks & Spencer.

Sprawled on a black leather sofa in his close-carpeted headquarters in the West End, novels and volumes of poetry competing for space with management texts on the bookshelves behind him, Dunn seems an unlikely entrepreneur. Most money men are willing to talk money all day, but Dunn is much happier when the conversation moves onto other matters, such as his love of sailing – he recently sold his two-and-a-half ton Bermudan sloop and is looking for another purchase – or his interest in the history of textiles, a way he has found of applying his scholarly bent to the world he has stumbled into. He buys ten different weeklies of varying political complexions and will often skim through two or three books in an evening's reading at home. But one should not underestimate how deeply he thinks about his business and business in general.

'Nobody at Oxford ever talked about business,' he says. 'The thing was to go into the professions or the civil service. Industry – trade it was called – was looked down on. It's something that we as a society need to change. Oxford and Cambridge and the public schools were set up to provide servants of the empire, but the empire is gone, the heartbeat of the country is now industry. That is the future. It is no longer the Battle of Waterloo that needs to be won on the playing fields of Eton but the economic war.'

Asked how Britain is doing in that war, Dunn shrugs. 'We have some very good businesses in this country,' he says. 'Marks & Spencer is a company which the whole world admires, but how many others like that do we have? Increasingly we are operating in a free world market, nobody owes Britain a living, we have to be competitive. It's not difficult, business is essentially simple, but the simple things have to be done well.'

Doing things well is Dunn's trademark. Less than four years after forming Tennyson, he is already ahead of a five-year plan which he thought when he made it was 'ridiculously ambitious'. The company is lean and hard. When he took over the average age of management was 61; now it is 34. Turnover last year was £1.1 million, more than double four years ago, with net profits of £126,000, and that was before the Marks & Spencer contract. As relaxed as he comes across, Dunn clearly doesn't like standing still. Last week he was in Germany buying pneumatic presses and high-speed sewing machines, and next month he goes to Sweden to see a new conveyor belt system that has been developed there.

'Marks & Spencer is perfect for us,' he says. 'We don't have to improve our conditions or quality control as we already share their values on such matters. They want to be cutting edge, so do we. And the fact that they are so demanding and so specific about what they want is perfect for me. I don't know anything about fashion, my knowledge is of production, and it means I can plan ahead, I don't have to worry about seasonality, I can keep my machines running at full capacity.'

A plan close to Dunn's heart is to start up a proper graduate trainee scheme, in the hope of attracting more men like him from Oxbridge. To provide him with some talented lieutenants? 'To take over from me, I hope,' he says. 'I can't see myself doing this for more than a few more years. I spent my childhood in Wales and I've always had a hankering to wander over my own hills talking to my sheep. Or if the business went the other way I would sell everything, buy a new boat and sail around the world.'

Helen

London, the Alps, the Caribbean

4th of October 1966

Dear Yeal,

Yes I will be your penpal. a friend at school Alice has a penpal from Denmark but Israil is further! Mummy says it is half a day on the aerplane did you get bord going home I would. Granma Golda is still sad alot. Mummy says she misses you and she still misses Grampa Eli tho they were always argewing when he was alive so I don't know. Robin and me always argew and I wouldn't miss him if he was in Timbucktew. Horridus sounds nice I wish we had a dog Daddy wants one but mummy said who will look after it she would end up that is why we have wellington. He is called wellington cos of his black boots. I would like to come to Tellaviv but Daddy doesn't want to go to Israil he prefers France.

Lots of love Helen

14th, June, '67

Dear Yael,

I hope you are alright and did not get bomed we saw on TV how children in Israel had to sleep in airaid shelters. Everyone here was very intrested in the war Daddy says the israeli army is the best in the world that they can win a whole war against much bigger armies in not even a week which is the first nice thing he has said about Israel so maybe we can come to visit you now. At school even the nonJews were talking about Israel and how brave it is. Did Uncle Naf shoot any arabs? I hope he is alright. It was lucky the avocadoes came before the war. I loved them they were my first ones so we are hopeing Uncle Naf's busniss is a big sucess and we can get more. Daddy says if he can corner the market he can make a bom which Robin thought meant a bom like in the war! We are going on a boat canaling in France with some friends in the holidays. (the Haslam's) They have a girl my age Harriet she is OK a bit boring and a boy for Robin. We went with them last year and I drove the boats alot of times. The engine conked out once just by a big weer we nearly crashed it was very funny.

Love Helen

My dear Yael, Thanks for the hunerka card I am sorry I didn't write back before I was so busy with Xmas then we came sking. I like sking but not classes. The cross is our

chaley. Merry new year and happy late birthday. Love
Helen.

April 28th, 1969

Dear Yael,

T U for your letter, you don't need to be sorry about your
English I am very impressed by it I can tell you. My Hebrew
is nonxistent the only word I can say is shalomb let alone
write any. I told my Dad I will have to start learning if I am
going to have a batmitsfer (is that how you spell it?) I got
rather keen on the idea since Mandy Green a friend at
school's older sister had one and got loads of watches,
money, record tokens etc. but it doesn't look like I am going
to have one as Dad doesn't approve of them. Actually he
doesn't approve of Hebrew cither he thinks Israel should
have chosen English, it was a big mistake according to him.
Don't worry Israel is not the only one we all make big mistakes in this house. I got your letter when we came back
from staying with some friends for Easter in Norfolk. We
had an Easter Egg hunt in the garden and went on long
walks and had hot toddys. Tomorrow I start my last term at
this school, next year I am going to an all girls school which
I am quite looking forward to too be honest as boys are very
annoying don't you think? I am sorry Uncle Naf has to go
into the army for so long is it forty days in the dessert or is
that the wrong religion? It sounds like you are very good at

tennis Dad tries to make me play but he always gets cross when I miss so now my ankle is permanently sprained.

Love Helen

Something I think it is still September '72
(I never know the date)

Dear Yael,

Its Saturday night and guess what am I out at a party or with friends? No. I am at home babysitting the brat while Mum and Dad have gone out galifanting as usual. Why they want to go out together I don't know as they always start shouting at each other even before they are out the door. God they get on my nerves sometimes, I wish I could emigrate. Maybe I will come to Tel Aviv, would you put me up?

Anyway I have put the brat in front of the TV so I can have some peace and write to you as it is two weeks since I got your letter; and I am feeling guilty. Yes we saw about the Israelis on TV; it was v. sad, and horrible of the Arabs to spoil the Olympics. Not that I am interested in sport in general but I loved the gynmastics; I was glued to the TV. God what I would give to be Olga Korbut. Did you watch her? Me and all my friends swooned over her I would have rushed out and started gynmastics straight away if I wasn't so fat and clumsy and could never in a million years be like that. Mum of course told me that it is not true I am very graceful but of course since she has started her pyschology course she can't be trusted to say what she really thinks and spends the whole time pyschologizing us, which of course drives Dad absolutely potty as he thinks it's all such crap.

I should tell you I am not completely sad; I did go to a dance at a school a couple of weeks ago and slow-danced and kissed with a boy who looked just like Marc Bolan, he is the lead singer of T. Rex, do you know them? They are my favourite group at the moment, they are truly brilliant. The boy was really nice, I wish I'd asked his name.

Your new house sounds really nice. Do you know when it will be ready? I am very jealous about the swimming pool.

I'd better go and make the brat go to bed.

Love,

Helen

Dear Yael, This is the beach we are on, it looks just like this, pretty cool, eh? We drink milk from coconuts and have seen the most beautiful fishes snorkelling. Actually I didn't know Marc Bolan was jewish, but anyway I am now into David Bowie. Ziggy Stardust is brilliant! I will write properly when I am home. Love Helen

October 17th, 1973

Dear Yael,

I hope you are alright. Israel is on the news every night and I look to see you though of course I hope I can't as they only show fighting, or usually anyway. Everyone says Israel will win. If you get bombed you can always jump in the swimming pool. I suppose that is a stupid thing to write. I can't imagine what it must be like, though I have to say sometimes it might as well be war in this house the way Mum and Dad are always losing their top. Though why I am writing about that when you are probably right now having to sit in an air-raid shelter I don't know. I have to say the Israeli soldiers on the news all look very gorgeous with their brown faces and guns. I can't remember if I was going out with Lazlo when I last wrote to you, anyway I have broken up with him and I met this really nice boy. His name is Sean, he is Irish, he has green eyes and a really nice per-sonality. We spent all evening kissing and him feeling my boobs, my neck was so covered in french kisses I've had to wear a blue polo-neck which I hate three days running. I am sure Mum has got it into her head that I like polo-necks, so I know what I will be getting for Xmas. Serves me right!

We heard about your tennis from somebody who wrote to Dad, I think they wanted some money from him, fat chance. You must be brilliant. Dad is really into tennis he takes Robin to play in the park on Saturday mornings. He tried to get me and Mum into it but we are on strike. Did you hear about that Ronnie Biggs chap losing at tennis to Billy Jean King? We women thought it was quite funny in this house I can tell you.

Probably you don't want to know any of this either, so I won't go on, I just wanted to say I am thinking of you.

Lots of love,

Helen

23 May '74

Dear Yael,

I am scribbling this so Aunt Zelda can take it with her when she goes back to Israel. She has come to lunch today. I think our family is quite a disappointment to her she is probably glad Grandma Golda is not alive to see us. We had to pretend that Robin is still 12 as she would have kittens that he didn't have a barmitzvah. She kept saying isn't he a very big boy for 12. Anyway, I hope you are fine. I am alright. I chucked Christian so I am single again. You don't think I am a tart do you? I'd better stop and put this in an envelope or Aunt Zelda will think I'm being rude hiding away.

Lotsa love,

Helen

3rd February 1975

Dear Yael,

How are you? I am sitting here desperately trying to learn my part for the school play. I am middle-aged spinster, v. cool eh? Or not. At least I get to pretend to be drunk. Talking of which, it was so embarrassing, Mum came back last night from her C. R. group totally sozzled. She practically couldn't stand up and had this inane grin on her face, you couldn't understand a word she was saying. If that is consciousness raising then I'm a banana. The only good thing was that Dad wasn't here as I'm sure they would have declared World War Three, but Wednesday is his Yorkshire night when he visits his factory up there. Or at least that's what he says, he probably has a Yorkshirean family. I swear every time he goes away Mum does something more outrageous or fills another bit of the house with her rubbish. Dad keeps threatening to make a great big bonfire but Mum's new explanation is that her hoarding is because her parents lost everything when they left Germany so she has anxiety about separation (from bits of paper!!??).

You see what a madhouse I live in!

Which brings me nicely to the subject of getting away and coming to Israel! I have written to the kibbutz people and Mum and Dad have agreed, if reluctantly on Dad's part as he thinks if I go to Israel I will almost certainly marry a rabbi or worse turn into one. (Can women be rabbis?) Anyway, the point is it looks like I will be coming, as long, of course, as I do not completely mess up my 'A' levels. When are you going to be in the army? Will we be able to get some time together?

Apart from that nothing has changed. I am still going out with Kwame but I don't think it will last, as I have discovered he is betrothed in marriage to some girl back in Ghana! That's about it, really. I'll let you know about the kibbutz etc. I am very excited about the prospect, I almost feel I have fallen for Israel already. Until then, my dear,

Mucho love

Hel

6 July 1976

Dear Yael,

As you can see here I am back home. How is Israel coping without me? Being home was alright for about a day or two, although my very first night Mum had to go out to some psycho meeting. Can you believe it? Her only daughter back after 6 months away and she can't even stay in for the night? Nothing has changed here. Mum has already told me three times that Dad is a Male Chauvenist Pig, twice in front of him, while Dad keeps raising his eyebrows at me to try and get me on his side. My view is that they are both meshuggah (!) Neither of them is the slightest bit interested in what I have been up to, once Dad had established I wasn't wearing a wig he didn't want to hear anything about Israel while Mum keeps asking me about Jewish customs. Yesterday she asked if I would like to have a Friday night supper! As if she even knows what to do. I told her she can do what she likes I am going out.

I have to do something to drown my sorrows. I feel like I am in exile since I left. I had the most romantic last few days in Tel Aviv, staying up late and sleeping half the day and then wandering down to the beach with the sleep still in my eyes. Hopefully Bjorn will be coming here before the end of the holidays and I've promised I'll go to Sweden at Xmas so this exile will not last forever, thank God.

Hey, what about Entebbe! Everyone was v. impressed, even the anti-semite as Mum calls him. (Dad.)

My love to everyone,

Hel

Julia

London, 1978

Hello, come in, come in, I'm Julia, Marion's friend. Happy
Passover. Do you say that? Happy Passover? Isn't it terrible
that I don't know? Have you done this before? If you have
it's more than me. Here, let me take your coat.

What's this? How nice of you.

Did you know that palwin symbolizes the blood from
circumcision? Not that that's what you want to be thinking
when you're drinking it, is it?

Marion? She's in the kitchen doing last minute stuff. There's
more to all this than the books make out.

Oh yes, we've been mugging up for weeks. We went down
to Jerusalem the Golden and bought an armful of books. Do
you know Jerusalem the Golden? In Golders Green? It's the
most wonderful shop, you really must go there. These two

tiny old Jewish men run it, you can't just walk in, you have to press the bell, they come and peer at you through the glass to make sure you're not PLO or something before they let you in. It's like an Aladdin's cave in there, they've got absolutely everything, books, candlesticks, shawls. I never even knew it existed, it's amazing what goes on in your own town without you realizing.

It's a very funny story actually. You know I work with Marion, well one day she mentioned it was Yom Kippur. I had no idea, I mean I barely knew what Yom Kippur was. I still don't really to be honest. I've read up on Passover but I haven't got onto Yom Kippur yet. It's the new year, isn't it? Or is that Rosh Hashanah? Oh, God, which is it? It is the New Year. No, it's the fasting one, that's right, Jack's mother was always going on about fasting for Yom Kippur. Well, anyway, Marion said it's Yom Kippur, so we decided to go out for tea to celebrate and that's when we had the idea to do a Seder.

Did you know in Morocco the Jews run up and down the streets shouting before the Seder meal? Or is it after? I read it in this book we got at Jerusalem the Golden about Seders through the Ages. It sounds rather fun, doesn't it, though I don't think Marion's neighbours would appreciate it.

–

My husband? God no, he's away. He always goes away this time of year. Come to think of it that must be why. The first couple of years we were married we went to Seders with his family, but after that we could never go because we were always away. It's never occurred to me before but that's the reason. Isn't he sly?

Oh yes. We've gone over the whole place for breadcrumbs with a fine-tooth comb. Or at least a hoover. We even put up a mezuzah, did you see it at the door? If you're really serious you're supposed to kiss it when you go in and out. You know the joke about the mezuzah, don't you?

Oh, it's hilarious. Now how does it go? There's a chap inside the mezuzah. No, that's not it. You must know it. Everyone knows it. Wait, wait, I've got it, that's right. There's this chap, he always wanted to know what's inside mezuzahs, finally he opens one there's a note saying, Help, I'm stuck in a mezuzah factory.

It's hilarious, isn't it?

Help, I'm stuck in a mezuzah factory.

Come along, everybody, it's time to sit down. The photocopies by each place are from the Haggadah, you can use your own if you've bought one, but we've edited these a little. I should just say something about the shank of lamb. It's very interesting actually, I've been reading up the history, Passover was originally a spring festival. All the bread business came in when the Jews were farmers but before that when they were nomads it was about the new-born lambs. That's why you're supposed to have a lamb shank. It's the sacrificial animal. Now what was I saying? Oh yes, the shank of lamb. Well, you are strictly supposed to have a roast shank of lamb but with Joan and Francis being vegetarian we've gone with a roast aubergine instead.

Come on everybody, you have to drink the wine, everyone's got to drink four glasses before the evening's out.

Oh, is that right?

Marion, did you hear that, you're supposed to have special small glasses so people don't get too drunk.

Oh well, never mind.

Yes, I was telling Joan, I did go to a couple, when I was first married, at Jack's aunt's but I was so busy trying not to make some terrible faux pas I didn't take in much. The first time it was awful, I had this terrible cold, I was meeting Jack there, he was coming from somewhere, I got there in a taxi, I was clutching a box of tissues, his Aunt Zelda opened the door and before I could stop her she automatically reached out and took the box of tissues saying how kind I shouldn't have, it was so embarrassing. But then Jack fell out with his uncle and we didn't go to any more.

262

Oh, he was working for his uncle, but then Jack wanted to go out on his own and his uncle was terribly upset. It caused this big family split that took years to heal.

My father's dead, but I did try to persuade my mother to come, you'd have thought I was trying to drag her into the gas chambers.

Ha, brilliant, brilliant.
Marion, did you hear what Alan said?
Pass the sacrificial aubergine.

Well Passover is a celebration of freedom isn't it, and that's what Marion's doing, celebrating her freedom from George. She says the two hundred and ten years the Jews were enslaved was nothing compared to her seventeen years of marriage.

My husband's at tennis camp, actually, somewhere in America. He's very keen on tennis.
No, well, a bit. I quite enjoy it really, but I'm terrible at it. I run around like a headless chicken shrieking. Jack bought me all the kit and sent me to lessons. He wanted me to play mixed doubles with him, it's an essential social skill in some circles you know, but the only time I played I let him down so badly we've never been invited again. You know what the form is, everybody is very jolly, saying good shot or well

played however badly you are actually playing but whenever we were at the back of the court Jack would be hissing at me to do this or stand there. In the end I had to pretend I'd sprained my ankle. Jack was furious, my marriage has never recovered.

No, no, I'm just joking.

I think I should explain that we have missed out a bit here from the reading, we decided that it was rather too strong really. All that stuff about pouring wrath on the nations that do not recognize God and removing them from under the skies, seemed a bit, well, you know, especially in the light of recent events. It was all seeming so hopeful after Sadat's visit, and now there's been this terrible tragedy with the bus and what's going on in Lebanon, but we mustn't dwell. Is it time to drink the next glass of wine?

No, my kids wouldn't come to something like this any more than their father. He spent their childhood indoctrinating them against it all. He wouldn't even let them read the Bible, he used to keep it on the top shelf like Playboy or something and bring it down to mock it to them, you know, making fun of all the begat begats and Noah having a son called Ham and how if you turn over two pages it says Cain was sick and then two pages later the lot fell on Abel?

Is that right?

The lot fell on Abel or was it that something fell on Lot?

Now about the songs, we've got a tape to sing along with. The words are all in the Haggadah but not the tunes so when we found this tape at Jerusalem the Golden we thought we could sing along to it the first time and if everybody really wants to afterwards we can try it without. Is that alright with everyone? Shall I put it on now?

Yes, we've got relations in Israel, but Jack won't go there even though it's his sister and her family. Naphtali is the person who introduced avocados to England. He bought up the avocado concession or something with the same legacy from Jack's great uncle that got Jack started. They used to hate each other but now they get on rather well when Ruth and Naphtali come to England.

Is that glass of wine going begging? If nobody's going to drink it I wouldn't –

It's what?

Oh, gosh, how embarrassing, I was about to drink the Cup of Elijah. This palwin does rather grow on you, though, doesn't it? Is there any left?

–

Well I think it was a great success, Marion, everybody had a wonderful time, we should be very proud of ourselves.

What did I say about George? I didn't mention George once all evening.

I was only repeating what you said.

What's the matter? Marion you're crying. What is it? Is it about George?

Oh, Marion, I didn't realize. You're really upset. I thought you were all right about it. Oh, Marion, I'm sorry, I've been a bad friend. I should have thought. It must be really hard for you with you and George, and me and Jack so happy.

Jerusalem

England

4th June, 1985. Down to the R-Ls for lunch and tennis.
Food B, wine B-. Perry Ashlington was there, debated with
him the delights of Mrs T. vs Tina Turner, the Negro singer
with the thighs. He for the Iron Lady, me for the iron
thighs. Met Jack Dunn, boss of Tennyson, a 'thrusting'
company according to Andrew. Dunn (original name?)
gives an impression of affability but he was tough as
brazils on the tennis court where with his new (-bile)
young wife he swept all asunder. Turned on my charm
with Polly? Lucy? at tea but she had eyes only for her
thrusting husband.

2nd July. Spotted a piece in today's Times about Jack Dunn's
(the tennis player) company Tennyson buying some bespoke
furniture makers. The share price was up 5%, a rise of

almost 100% since the company floated last year. Note: look into shares.

28th July. To Glyndebourne with Daphne and the Palmers to see Willard White in Porgy & Bess. V. stirring. Bess in particular v. striking and sensuous indeed. Entranced. Bumped into Jack Dunn in the interval. He was with some sponsored tent. Agreed to have lunch after the hols. Assumptions about Dunn's origins rather thrown off by his remarkable resemblance to W. White.

30th July. Dunn's secretary called to arrange lunch.

12th Sept. V. good lunch at Savoy with Jack Dunn. Food A-. Wine A+. He ordered an excellent vintage claret from some small vineyard have never heard of. Must remember to get the name from him. Is Hebe as presumed (Dunnowitz?) but not mafia sort. Surprisingly good company. He told a v. funny joke about a dentist who runs out of anaesthetic so gets his nurse to jab the patient in the bottom as a distraction as he pulls out his tooth, the patient yells, the dentist asks if he is OK, the patient says yes he just didn't realize the roots went that deep. Come to think of it could that have been some ethnic reference? Anyway – his story is that he read Law at Oxford but his heart was never really in it and when he went up to the Bar and found he would have to wait around for his Oxford 'chums' to qualify as solicitors and start sending him briefs he jumped ship at the first opportunity which turned out to be an uncle's shmuttah business and the rest is history. Told him not to apologize, shmuttah is a more noble profession than law any day. Barristers are all vultures. He is v. bullish about his business. Must call broker tomorrow.

16th November. Tennyson up another 30p after buying LMG, a Classical music recording co. Have made 12% in two months. Should have bought more shares.

15th February, 1986. To the Dunnowitzes for supper. Food and wine A/A+. Sat next to Penny wife of Larry Soames, v. boring, and Leona something or other, a friend of Lucy, who sung Jack's praises, he's done marvels for Lucy, though she's done marvels for him too, he was trapped in miserable marriage etc . . . Entertained self by drinking too much and watching Leona's ample breasts and thighs quiver. The house is hung with v. expensive and beautiful old textiles. Lucy explained this is a hobby of Dunn's. They looked museum quality.

23rd March. Feeling quite proud of self. Dunnowitz has been appointed a trustee of the V&A. Simon T. is ecstatic to get on board such a shrewd businessman and expert on antique textiles to boot, while Dunn rang to say thank you for the recommendation so I am in his good books too, which might bring some reward.

3rd May. Good lunch at Claridges with Dunnowitz yesterday. We are getting to be quite pally. He explained Tennyson's acquisitions philosophy: buying up businesses which he is either a customer of or would like to be a customer of. He is v. pleased with the V&A, says there is a lot to be done there, told him that's why he's there. He's in Oxford getting an honorary fellowship from his old college today which he said is ironic as what he really wanted was to be an English don but they wouldn't let him change from Law.

17th June. Recovering from weekend at the Dunnowitzes country residence. Little Foldwell, village on the Glous/Ox border. A fine Regency vicarage, v. tastefully done. Beautiful gardens. Dunn proudly showed off the folly where Harold Witherington supposedly wrote Vicar of Peridge. Never read it, tripe probably. More interesting was his glorious mint condition Bristol 403. Went for a spin in it, in heaven. Only 13 000 miles on clock. It must have cost him a mint. Dunn said he couldn't resist, that he always wanted to be racing driver. Racing-driving English don? Lots of activities – tennis both mornings with the host and hostess vanquishing all comers fiercely and apologetically and a long walk Saturday afternoon with the pedigree labradors. As we were walking past the village church this awful home counties sort practically sprinted out to simper over Dunn, the whole village can't thank him enough for the money for the church roof. She invited him to open the village fete. Must get him to contribute to Ugandan school.

3rd July. Three thousand squid for school from Dunnowitz!

22nd November. Dinner party at Tony P's. Horrible evening. Trapped next to this nightmarish man-hating feminist harpie. Everything I said she harangued me about. She psychoanalyst (good phrase that: 'she-psychoanalyst'!). My every harmless comment was twisted by her in typical psycholooney fashion. Told her my theory about the whole thing being a con as it applies only to the neurotic middle-class Hebes Freud studied in Vienna and she accused me of anti-semitism of all things. Defended myself vigorously by rolling up the flag for Israel and telling her my theory that only Foreign Office Lawrence-type bugger boys and lefty looneys are Arabists but she even gave me a dirty look about that. Only at the end did I discover that she was Dunnowitzes ex-wife! No wonder he left her. Nice legs, though.

12th July, 1987. Watched Martina win Wimbledon again on the box. Not the beauty she was when she first appeared on scene as a luscious 18-yr-old but still fine limbed. Spotted the Dunnowitzes in the crowd.

3rd November. Tennyson shares down 20% in two weeks. Called Dunnowitz in a panic. He is unconcerned, says they were overvalued anyway and the company is in a strong position: no borrowings, cash in bank and that what people want in a recession is classic products, quality, value for money. He said that every crisis is an opportunity.

Ecclesiastes

Little Foldwell, 1990

Oh, shit.

Tel Aviv

Tel Aviv, 1996

Shalom, everybody, thank you very much for being here and giving your support to our country's young tennis players. Before I introduce our special guest who is going to present the prizes, I would like to say a few brief words. I do hope you have all enjoyed the tournament, which I think I can rightly say has been a big success. Thank you also to everybody who has made a contribution. If we are to regain a place in the upper reaches of world tennis we are going to have to invest further in our young players. It was only a few years ago that in Shlomo Glickstein and Amos Mansdorf we had two players in the top hundred in the world and a competitive team in the Davis Cup, but since then our standards have sadly declined somewhat, though I must offer my congratulations to this year's Davis Cup team who played so well to defeat Norway in the first round of the Euro/African

Zone Group One before suffering a plucky defeat against a strong Spanish side in round two. As I was saying if we want to produce further players of the standard of Glickstein and Mansdorf we need to create an environment in which champions can be nurtured. If Pete Sampras, who I am sure you all know is half-Jewish, had grown up here, I wonder if we would have had the facilities and encouragement to have set him on the path to being world champion? It is a good question and the answer is perhaps not. But now I do believe we are putting in place the necessary network to make the most of our young tennis talent, many of whom you have seen here over the past few days. I don't want to bore you any more, so let me now introduce our special guest, a man who himself is no stranger to challenges on the tennis court, having fought back from a near fatal heart attack while playing tennis some years ago to wielding a racket again most competitively, as I discovered myself in a game of mixed doubles yesterday evening. He is also the great uncle of one of our most promising youngsters, Etan Goldblatt, who is currently ranked twenty-eighth in the under-ten age group. Ladies and gentlemen, a man who has been most generous in his support of the Israel Tennis Association for the past five years, Mr Jack Dunn, CBE.

Circumlocution

London, 2001

God, Robin and me had the funniest time trying to decide. I mean it was bizarre. I suppose we had always assumed we would do it, but then, well, when you actually think about what it involves it seems so barbaric. And it's not as though we do anything else. I mean okay my parents had Friday nights at home but only when I started going out in the evenings and they stopped as soon as my brothers and I left home. As for Robin I don't think he's been in a synagogue in his life. It's against his religion. I mean the only Jewish ritual we perform is going to the new Woody Allen film when it comes out. Anyway, at the time we were going to this NCT class in Hendon. You know how it is, they assign you to the nearest class, we didn't think anything about it but when we turned up it was a Jewish NCT class. I mean not officially but the woman who ran it was this complete frummer, with the wig and everything, and everyone there was Jewish. Well, there was one couple who weren't but they didn't come back after the first time and this other woman we suspected wasn't but she kept pretty quiet and if you grow up in north London it's pretty easy to, you know, pass. You tend to think of Orthodox Jews as living in the dark ages but this woman was all up with the NCT stuff – natural childbirth, no drugs, water births, practising your breathing, husband being there, and we'd been agonizing over you know what so we thought we'd bring it up in class and, God, it was like, I don't know, we'd said we were thinking about eating the baby when it came. There was this intake of breath likes snakes hissing and then we were under attack from all sides. Didn't we know about the penile cancer rates if you didn't do it? And the cervical cancer rates. And what it was like if a boy had to have it done later in life. This one woman said in this hoity-toity voice that the Royal Family did it and if it was good enough for them it was good enough for her as if we were insulting the Queen. And the frummer woman wouldn't even talk about it. I mean she just refused. All we wanted was the medical facts to help us decide but the truth is it's impossible to get the facts. We tried everything. We asked our GP, we looked it up on the net. We thought we'd found this reasonable article but it turned out it was written by Dr Levi Mandlebaum or something from the Jewish Hassidim Hospital in New York. Even my midwife was the same. I had an awful labour, I won't go into it, but I ended up two days later on an epidural completely exhausted and finally with this lovely Nigerian midwife. We were sitting there waiting for the oxytocin or whatever it's called to kick in and bring on my contractions and we realized we still hadn't decided so we thought we'd ask her what she thought and blow me down if she wasn't the bloody mohel or whatever it is in Ibo for the Nigerian community in London and was all for chopping any little boy she could get her hands on. The truth is, deciding is a political issue. Or at least cultural or something. It all seems so simple at the beginning. You're Jewish. Your husband is done and you want your child to be the same. But once you look into it, well, did you know that in America men have started suing their parents for doing it to them, and trying to reverse it? They tie things to what's left to pull it down or have operations to replace it. It's true. You start going round in circles. Yes, okay, it's a statement of who you are, but how right is it to label your child in that way? Did you see that film about the Jewish boy who tried to pass himself off as Hitler Youth to save his life and every time he needed to pee he risked his life? Well I mean it is the kind of thing you think about when you're pregnant and you can't sleep in the middle of the night isn't it? All right that's the past and it's never going to happen again, touch wood, or touch trees, jungles, the Brazilian rain forest. I mean look at what's happening now in Israel.

You know apart from when my father took us all to Raid on Entebbe – it was the only film he ever took us to, it was an appalling film, but it was like watching your team win the cup final, everyone in the audience was clapping and cheering and weeping – apart from then I've never felt very involved with Israel. It's always seemed so far away, like a cousin you never see, but now, God, I watch the pictures on television, or to be honest I don't watch them, I find them too painful. I mean, this isn't what Jews are meant to be like, is it? Robin says Israel took two main things out of the holocaust, one that the Jews must never be weak again, always be strong, the other that because of what they had witnessed they were sort of the conscience of the world, and when Israel had to be strong it did it reluctantly, with a heavy heart. But now the being strong seems to have won, the conscience has been shouted down. I mean, what does everyone else think?

Decide what?

Oh, that, I had a girl, Becky.

Acknowledgements

This novel is a magpie's work. Writing it I have pilfered glittery bits from too many people, books and other sources to mention. I am beholden to all of them and I hope I have not taken too many liberties.

I owe a big debt of gratitude to Clare Alexander. My thanks also to Ben Ball; to Henry; and to Leah, Jemima and, especially, Judy.